Just as his heart softened—
her will hardened . . .

The viscount, who had thought he could not leave fast enough, had found, in the last two weeks, that he had little inclination to leave the Carrington home at all. Now the reason for his turnabout in attitude calmly sat telling him that she had written his family and asked that they remove him.

"My lord?"

The viscount realized Miss Carrington was looking at him questioningly just as he realized his mouth was hanging open, and he closed his jaws with a snap.

"Well!" he said. "I did not realize my presence here was so repugnant to you that you could not *wait* to be rid of me!"

"Repug—" Julia started to repeat the word, as if stunned, then shook her head. "Oh, no," she said, holding out one hand almost beseechingly. "Your presence here—well, after the first week, anyway—has been *far* from repugnant! But it cannot go on . . ."

Titles by Judith Nelson from Jove

THE ACCIDENTAL MATCH
INSTRUCTING ARABELLA
TWO HEARTS TRUMP

The Accidental Match

Judith Nelson

JOVE BOOKS, NEW YORK

All the characters in this book are fictitious, and any resemblance to actual persons, living or dead, is purely coincidental.

THE ACCIDENTAL MATCH

A Jove Book / published by arrangement with
the author

PRINTING HISTORY
Jove edition / November 1995

ISBN: 0-515-11749-8

A JOVE BOOK®
Jove Books are published by The Berkley Publishing Group,
200 Madison Avenue, New York, New York 10016.
JOVE and the "J" design are trademarks
belonging to Jove Publications, Inc.

PRINTED IN THE UNITED STATES OF AMERICA

10 9 8 7 6 5 4 3 2 1

This book is for Chuck and Anna,
who loved to laugh.
Both gone too soon.

The Accidental Match

Chapter
One

The lane was overgrown and rutted and, in the quickly gathering gloom, the trees on either side cast deep shadows that made it difficult to see. The gentleman in the well-sprung phaeton compressed his lips when one of his wheels fell into a rut, and his dark face was as stormy as the threatening sky above him.

This was all Arabella's fault, he thought, his eyes smoldering while he pretended his long fingers were as expertly wrapped around his loving sister-in-law's neck as they were around the reins that held his high-strung team in check. If she hadn't been so determined to see him wed, parading debutante after debutante beneath his nose despite his alternately reasonable arguments and vociferous objections, and the milder arguments and objections of her husband, he would not now be on this road.

At thought of the lady's husband, his brother, the gentleman's eyes narrowed further. This was Charles's fault, too, he decided.

It was Charles who had married Arabella. And now that interfering female, so happy in her own marriage and motherhood, was doggedly determined to see her brother-in-law Jack as happily wed.

1

She turned a deaf ear to Jack's protestations that he would rather be drowned than leg shackled, and steadfastly refused to believe that any man could be happy without a wife. A wife, she told him, would give his mind a better turn, and would distract him from some of his more dangerous pursuits.

"Ha!"

Jack said the word aloud, his dark eyes snapping at her temerity. His mind was turned quite well, thank you, and he enjoyed his pursuits—the more dangerous, the better. Far better to be in danger than sitting in someone's receiving room about to expire from the ennui of conversation with some beautiful ninny or her dragon of a mother who had no more to say to him than "Oh, yes, my lord; oh, no, my lord, do you really think so, my lord? La, you are naughty, my lord!"

Jack shook his head with distaste and, forgetting where he was for a moment, let his hands drop. His team took instant advantage, lengthening their stride, and he pulled them up sharply. Jack might be careless of his own safety but he was never careless of his horses, and he did not want them injured by this cow path of a road he had taken in the hope it would more quickly bring him to the small but excellent inn where he planned to spend the night.

Casting another glance toward the sky he all but resigned himself to a good drenching. That would be the perfect capstone to this all-things-gone-wrong day.

Arabella had lured him to his grandfather's house in London that morning where she, his grandfather the earl, and his brother, Charles, were spending the season by the simple expedient of sending him a note requesting his presence immediately.

The note had hinted that she needed his help, even if it had not stated that directly, so what could he do but attend?

She was, after all, his sister-in-law, and such a minx that Jack had no trouble believing she had done something she did not want to have come to Charles's ears. Of course in such an instance she would seek aid from Jack. Jack had done a few things he did not wish to ever have come to Charles's ears, either, and Arabella was shrewd enough to know that.

Plus, there were times—not lately, but there *were* times— that Jack was genuinely fond of the girl, for she had made his brother inordinately happy, and when Charles had added her to their small family by marrying her, Jack had admitted her to *his* heart, as well.

Since Jack guarded his heart zealously, she had overcome no small obstacle to make herself a place there.

So, if Arabella actually was in some kind of trouble—if she'd spent her pin money already and overextended herself, or if she'd lost more than she wanted Charles to know about at cards, for the lady did love to gamble—Jack would feel bound to help her out of her fix (all the while ringing a rare peal over her head, of course!)

So Jack had gone in answer to her summons. He had gone like a lamb to the slaughter, for upon arriving at the earl's home at the time Arabella had set, he found not just his sister-in-law awaiting him in her drawing room, but other females, as well.

Young females.

Young, unmarried females.

Lady Jane Dimpleton, who laughed like a horse. Miss Wraxton, with her long, thin nose and her pale blond hair and her cold blue eyes and her interminable conversation of lineage—her own, of course. Miss Browning, who played the harp. *The harp!* And their mothers. Women with big bosoms and narrowed eyes, who knew to the penny and the acre what Jack would inherit with his grandfather's title. Women who knew all there was to know about the marriage mart.

The day grew darker by the moment and the wind was chill, but Jack felt a trickle of sweat run down his neck as he remembered the scene. He had made good his escape only when his unsuspecting brother entered the room to inform Arabella that Charles and the earl were going out. Evincing surprise at finding Jack there, Charles asked if his brother had come to see their grandfather. Jack had seized on that remark as a drowning man seizes a rope, and had said that yes, yes, he must see the earl at once, he had something of great importance to discuss with him.

Ignoring Charles's look of mild surprise and Arabella's clear suspicion, Jack had frowned heavily at his sister-in-law, a frown that threatened grave retribution, and had quit the room. In the library he inquired if there was anything the earl wished from his country estate—anything at all—and upon hearing that there were a few papers the old man wished he had brought with him to town, Jack volunteered to retrieve them. Immediately.

Charles, who had followed his brother into the library at a more leisurely pace, said he was surprised to hear Jack wished to leave London now, at the height of the season. Jack glared at him.

"I don't *wish* to leave London," Jack had said. "I *must*, to preserve my sanity. And to keep me from murdering your wife! That infernal parade of unattached females she insists on foisting on me is beyond bearing, Charles! Everywhere I go, there she is, with another young ninny in tow! Did you see the collection she had in there today? Miss *Browning!*"

"The harp!" Charles responded, appalled; all three gentlemen shuddered.

An apologetic Charles said he would speak again to his wife; he already had forbidden her from interfering in Jack's life, and he would do so again.

"Well," Jack huffed. "We see how well she attends to *you*."

Charles had smiled—the doltish smile of a man in love, Jack had thought, revolted—and said that his wife attended to him very well; she just did as she pleased, no matter what he said.

Jack followed that disgusting comment with a deeply held and impassioned response concerning a wife's duties to her husband. He had ended his response abruptly when he saw the broad smiles growing on both his brother's and grandfather's faces—smiles they made no efforts to hide.

Driving along now, lost and cold and likely at any moment to be wet, as well, Jack thought they could at least have tried to hide their amusement.

Say what they might, Jack had no doubt that *his* wife would behave just as he thought she should, and would do his every bidding—*if* he took a wife, which he had no intention of doing for years and years, if ever. Let the succession go to Charles and Charles's son, Jack.

At thought of the baby named for him the gentleman smiled in spite of himself, then turned the collar up on his great coat in an effort to gain a little more protection from the wind. Perhaps he should not have set off from London so late in the day, he thought, then gave a grim grin as he realized he was echoing his man Phipps's words. It was always so irritating when Phipps was right.

After Jack's short conversation with his grandfather he had hastened to his own London home to tell his valet to throw several shirts, his shaving gear, and an extra coat and a pair of buckskins into his portmanteau while Jack sent word to the stables to have his phaeton brought round immediately.

Mr. Phipps, that excellent man who had been with him nearly three years, accorded that command the smile it deserved, and asked his lordship what it was he wished, *really*, and where they might be going, so Mr. Phipps could make appropriate clothing preparations. Jack frowned at him.

"*I*," Jack said, enunciating the word carefully, "am driving down to High Point for a few days. By myself. Alone. There are no 'clothing preparations' to make. I shan't be keeping company, and I shan't be going out. Now do as I say, and be quick about it!"

Phipps had stared at him in amazement. "Going out of town, my lord?" the man repeated, as if the idea were foreign to him. "Without *me?*"

The way Phipps uttered the last phrase had brought a sardonic grin to Jack's face. "Without you, Phipps," his lordship agreed. "I'm taking the phaeton, and I don't need you squeezed in beside me, heaving your martyr sighs!"

At sight of his valet's face the viscount's eyebrows rose. "What? Don't you think I can dress myself?"

Phipps, being polite to a fault, had kept to himself the private but firmly held belief that his lordship certainly could not. Instead he said, with real nobility of character, that he would not mind riding in the phaeton, if that was his lordship's wish. He would not mind at all.

"But *I* would," Jack said, pulling on his gloves and

preparing to leave the room. "I would mind a great deal. I leave in fifteen minutes. Have my bag ready!"

In fifteen minutes, to the second, Phipps, his nose in the air, had descended the stairs of Jack's London house, the portmanteau held rigidly in his grasp, every fiber of his being making it clear just how outrageous he found his master's behavior. Jack, standing by the front door, almost ready to depart, grinned when he saw him, and crossed the hall to take the bag, saying as he did so, "Oh, give over Phipps, do. It's an unexpected holiday for you, not a sentence to the guillotine!"

Phipps sniffed. "If, my lord, my service has not been satisfactory, and if, my lord, you no longer require my service—"

"Your service is far above satisfactory, as you very well know," the viscount had interrupted. "And you can lay the fact that I wish to go off by myself in this way to an obvious blemish on my character, not yours. That should make you happy."

Phipps was heard to say that a blemish on his lordship's character was something he could not now or ever be happy about, and Jack rolled his eyes.

"I am only glad," Jack had said, "that John is gone this afternoon, so I don't have to listen to a bear jaw from him, too."

The valet was so offended that his employer considered his comments a bear jaw that he could barely speak, but he brightened after a moment as his eyes fell upon the undergroom who was holding the exceedingly fresh team hitched to Jack's phaeton at the bottom of the stairs. Remembering that his lordship's excellent groom, who had been with Jack ever since the young man was breeched, was away for the afternoon, and would be even more affronted than his lordship's valet was at being left behind, Phipps realized that to him would fall the pleasure of telling the man.

Noting Phipps's brightening expression, Jack grinned. "Yes, you may tell him," Jack said, "and the two of you will no doubt have a comfortable time ripping me to shreds."

"If you wish to joke, my lord—" Phipps began, but it was clear to Jack that the man was already anticipating just such a convivial time.

"The joke, Phipps, is that long face of yours," the viscount had returned. "And it will do you no good to poker up on me again like that, because I'm going without both of you. I am running away from people who try to tell me what to do, Phipps—and you may tell John so, and watch him frown! And what's more, I'm going to enjoy this time by myself, too!"

Now, as Jack felt a raindrop hit his face, followed in short order by another, it occurred to him that the joke was not on Phipps or John, but on himself. From the time he was a young boy his grandfather and brother had told him he was too headstrong by half, and now look where his temper had gotten him.

Hunching his shoulders and thinking longingly of warm hands and a well-chosen supper, he rounded a bend in the lane just as two small shapes darted from the steep ditch to his left and raced into the center of the road.

"Children!" Jack whispered the word, and his eyes grew wide as he saw them standing as if frozen as his team bore down on them.

Hauling on the reins with all his might, Jack might have carried off the rescue without harm to anyone if a wheel hadn't caught in one of the ruts on the side of the road as the horses plunged forward and back. For a brief moment the phaeton seemed to hang suspended on the left wheel.

Jack tried in desperation to throw his weight to the right, willing the vehicle to straighten, but as he rose to make his move the horses plunged again, throwing him off-balance, and out of the phaeton as it fell. Jack had the strangest sensation of flying—not at all unpleasant, just odd—and he had only a split second to look to see that the children appeared unharmed, and had moved out of the team's way; were, in fact, staring at him openmouthed and with fright in their eyes, before he landed in the ditch. His head struck a stone there, and Jack gave up thinking in favor of darkness.

It was sound that awoke him, and Jack frowned. Somewhere a boy's voice was saying, "I've seen to the horses, Jules," and Jack thought if he could get no better room than this at the inn, where he must be subjected to hearing about every order obeyed by the hostlers, he would never stay in this place again. "One nasty knock to the hock, but we should be able to poultice it so you'd never know."

Jack wondered whose cow-handed driving had injured a team, then frowned slightly. Why was it so hard to open his eyes this morning? Had he made a batch of it last night? He tried to remember, but remembering was hard when the boy kept interrupting his thoughts.

A sudden change in the boy's voice made Jack frown again, for it contained a new excitement as the young man said, "Do you know who that is, Jules? Do you? It's Viscount Chalmsy! I saw him when I was up in London with Uncle William! He's a goer, Jules! Top of the trees! Sets the pace for everyone!"

Jack's frown deepened at the impertinence of a hostler describing him so; then it occurred to him that it was the *height* of impertinence, because what was a hostler doing in his room? He'd have to—to—

Once again the viscount's thoughts were interrupted as another voice, this time a very soft, feminine one, asked in a troubled tone, "Do you mean he is a lord, then, Edward?"

Edward assured her emphatically that he was. "Top of the trees, I told you, Cressy! Top of the trees!"

"Oh, dear," said the soft voice, making Jack's forehead furrow slightly at the troubled tone. "The children have killed a lord. That's very bad, I'm sure."

"Oh, for goodness' sake, Cressida!" A third, brisk voice entered the conversation, and Jack tried to puzzle out what all these people were doing in his room, or directly under his window. "It's no worse to kill a lord than to kill anyone— not that he's dead, for he is not, and you ought to be ashamed of yourself for scaring the children so!"

A contrite Cressida was heard to murmur that she was very sorry, she was sure; she hadn't meant to scare the children. Still, she couldn't help but dispute dear Julia's statement that killing a lord wasn't worse than killing anyone else; she was sure it was, quite sure. . . .

In this opinion she was seconded by young Edward, who was sure killing a lord must be ten times worse than killing anyone else, and killing Viscount Chalmsy would be the biggest crime of all.

The viscount, who agreed most emphatically with the last statement, frowned when it was dismissed with a brisk, "Nonsense! Murder is murder, and a terrible thing it is, too, be it a lord murdered, or a woodcutter! But I tell you, he is not dead, far from it! Look, he's coming around now!"

It was with real effort that Jack opened his eyes, for the

sole purpose of informing the person names Jules, or Julia—surely he had not heard the first name right!—that it was a bad thing, a very bad thing, to murder a lord, especially this one, but the sight that met his eyes made him flinch and quickly close them again.

"Oh, no," he muttered, his words caught only by the person kneeling close to his head as he uttered them. "I *am* dead. And this is heaven."

That person smiled, and shook her head. "No, my lord, you are not dead. And from what my brother suggests of your behavior, you might know very well that this isn't heaven!"

"*Jules*!"

Viscount Chalmsy heard two voices gasp as he opened his eyes again, a frown between his brows. This time, however, a quite different vision greeted his gaze; it was met and held by a brown-haired woman with a great deal of strength in her face, and a laugh in her brown eyes.

"But—" Jack objected, "you're—you're—"

"Julia Carrington," the woman supplied for him, reaching down and touching his unresisting hand as it rested on his chest.

"You're not the angel!" he finished. One of her mobile eyebrows rose, and she sighed even as her lips quirked up.

"Cressida," he heard her say, and he realized hers was the brisk voice in the earlier conversations. "Come bend over this unfortunate gentleman and assure him that you are flesh and blood, and that he has not departed this earth. I have things to do."

With that the brown-haired head disappeared, to be replaced in a moment by a blond, blue-eyed beauty with roses in her cheeks and a sympathetic smile.

"Does it hurt very badly?" the beauty asked, her voice musical. Jack looked up at her in confusion.

"Does what hurt?" he demanded, trying to move. It occurred to him suddenly that he was lying on the ground, which was really quite damp, and the blond vision was kneeling beside him. That was odd. Very, very odd.

"Your poor head," the young woman responded, using two small hands to press him back when he tried to rise. "You have quite a bump upon it."

"I have?" Jack repeated, gingerly feeling the area she indicated. He winced at the pain his gentle groping produced there, and the lady winced in response.

"Yes, quite a bump." The voice he now identified as belonging to Julia Carrington agreed, behind him. Jack couldn't help but note that Julia Carrington's voice held far less sympathy, and that thought rankled. "I think there's no lasting harm. You appear to me to be hardheaded enough for two lords!"

"Julia, please!" The tone was scandalized and young Edward moved into view, smiling apologetically down at the viscount as he assured his lordship that Edward's sister hadn't meant that the way it sounded.

"Oh?" With difficulty Jack raised one eyebrow toward Miss Carrington, who returned the look with a raised eyebrow of her own. "Somehow I doubt that!"

The lady did not blush or offer an apology. Her lips quirked upward and she gave a slight shrug as she changed the subject by saying, "Your horses have sustained some bruises, and one nasty hock, but if you come along to Carrington Place I am sure we can have them fit in no time."

"My horses . . ."

Again Jack frowned, trying to remember how his horses could have been injured. Suddenly it came to him.

"There were children!" Jack exclaimed, trying to rise and falling back with an exclamation of pain. Julia Carrington was beside him in a moment, her eyes narrowed as she gently touched the bump on his head and, not finding the cause for his collapse there, moved her hand firmly down his side—to his considerable chagrin—starting at his shoulder and not stopping until she reached his left ankle.

"Miss Carrington, really!" Jack said, catching her wrist and causing her to look up at him in surprise. When she saw the viscount's heightened color she did her best not to grin. There was a definite look about the man that suggested he would be much more comfortable moving his hand down a woman's thigh than having a woman do the same to him, even if the lady was checking for injuries, and the movement quiet innocent.

"I believe you have badly injured your ankle," Miss Carrington said gravely, letting not a hint of amusement show in her voice.

She removed her hand from his grasp to probe that afflicted area firmly while he gritted his teeth and felt the sweat start on his forehead. The lady frowned as Jack bit back a groan and reached for her wrist again.

"Never mind my ankle," the viscount said testily, "It will do very well, thank you. There is no reason for you be prodding at me, none at all, and I wish you to stop immediately. Attend to what is important, now! There were children in the road. Are they all right? Were they hurt in any way?"

Julia looked at him in surprise, and thought the better of him for asking. "No, Viscount Chalmsy, they were not injured," she said. "Your quick thinking turned your team in time. William, Lily—"

Miss Carrington waved a hand in the air and, as if conjured by magic, two youngsters, perhaps ages six and eight, appeared at her side and gazed down at the viscount. "Your apologies, please."

"We are very sorry, sir," began the older of the two manfully, his sturdy shoulders back as he uttered the words. "We should not have run into the road without listening and looking to see if there was anyone coming. We hope—we hope—"

What the boy hoped was never learned, for his smaller sister, after looking at the viscount fearfully, astounded that gentleman by casting herself upon his chest and sobbing there.

"Please don't die!" Jack heard the little girl plead into his great coat as she did her best to wrap her arms all the way around him. "Please, please don't die!"

Chapter Two

Viscount Chalmsy, who had sustained a nasty shock at awakening to find himself lying in a ditch with all these strange people around him, his ankle doing its best to compete with his throbbing head—to say nothing of the other aches and pains he was starting to feel, lying on the cold, wet ground—sustained another now.

Not only did the child's energetic hurling of herself onto his chest jar his injuries, causing him to flinch in spite of himself—a flinch Miss Carrington saw immediately, and frowned over—but he had no idea what to do when a six-year-old attached herself to him and wailed at the top of her lungs, such situations never before having come his way. At home in the ballroom and the boxing ring, on a field of honor and in the drawing rooms of London, the viscount was nonplussed in this situation.

Passing the question under rapid review, Viscount Chalmsy could not remember anyone ever begging him not to die with such fervor, and while he was pleased with the concern as a whole, having no desire to die himself, he was more than a little taken aback by the intensity with which the request was expressed.

"No, no," he said, trying to sit up, a task considerably hampered by the little girl lying on top of him. "Not at all."

He gave her back several awkward pats, hoping to comfort her, and was even more dismayed to find that that action, far from providing the relief he had hoped for, only caused the child to cry harder, and to tighten her hold. He raised frantic eyes toward Miss Carrington, who was reaching for Lily even before he did so.

"There, there, Lily," he heard the brown-haired woman say as she gently but firmly untangled the child's arms from the viscount's neck and lifted her sister's small body onto her hip, allowing the child to bury her face in Miss Carrington's shoulder. "You haven't killed the man, and you mustn't drown him, either! I imagine he's wet enough as it is!"

At the viscount's look of inquiry Miss Carrington explained that it had rained while he had been—she paused, looking down at the child in her arms, and amended what she had been about to say—asleep.

Jack was so astounded at the thought of being rained on and not knowing it that he did not note her careful choice of words, and asked how long he had been unconscious. Lily, whose sobs had been quieting, grew louder, and Miss Carrington frowned at him even as she said, "Long enough for the children to run to Carrington Place to tell us what happened, and for us to make the journey back."

The lady did not put a time to that and, the way she was glaring at him, the viscount did not think it best to inquire further. He watched as she shifted the child slightly on her hip and said in her brisk voice, "Now, now, Lily! The gentleman will be good as new in a trice, and so will you! Dry your tears and beg the viscount's pardon, for you wouldn't want him to think you have no more manners than Toby, would you?"

The viscount had no idea who Toby was, but the smiles

that came to Edward's, William's and Cressida's faces, as well as the watery chuckle that escaped from the small head buried in Miss Carrington's shoulder, convinced him that he had no desire to meet said Toby, in any circumstances.

"I'm sorry."

Jack heard the soft words and looked up into the two brown eyes still swimming with tears. The little girl had Julia Carrington's eyes and the golden hair of the sister he'd thought was an angel, Jack noted, and he had no doubt that she would grow up to be a beauty, too. He smiled.

"Quite all right," Jack said, executing a half bow that was hard to do in his current position, and made his head swim alarmingly. He was rewarded for his pain by a small smile on Lily's face that was reflected on Miss Carrington's.

"And you won't die?"

Jack was baffled by the anxiousness in the child's tone, and by the shadow that passed over Miss Carrington's face as she transferred the child to the young woman she'd earlier called Cressida.

"Word of honor," Jack said, smiling at the little girl. "I'll be right as can be in no time, you'll see."

He was rewarded with two dazzling smiles this time, one on the child's face and the other on the face of the angel.

"How nice," he heard Cressida approve softly, and his own smile widened. A chance glance to the left brought the eldest Miss Carrington's face into view, and the expression there made him realize he was grinning like an idiot.

The viscount's grin vanished and Miss Carrington, accurately reading the action, said practically, "Yes, well, we don't want you catching pneumonia while you're getting over your ankle and that head bump, so perhaps we'd better get you up off the ground and into the wagon, and take you off to Carrington Place to patch you up properly. Edward, lend a hand."

The lady started forward and Jack, realizing her intention to lift and support him, along with the aid of the young man he surmised was her brother since there was a strong resemblance between them and the lady had no trouble telling the young man what to do, forestalled her with a wave of his hand.

"No, no," Jack said, trying again to rise and feeling the sweat break out on his forehead as he did so, "there is no need—"

He fell back, very pale, and Miss Carrington informed him with a tartness reminiscent of his first governess that there was every need; she didn't want to have to carry his dead weight to the wagon, which they would have to do if he continued in this foolish manner and fainted on them, so he could just mind his manners and let them help him.

"*Jules!*" breathed a scandalized Edward, and his sister looked at him in surprise.

"Well?" Julia questioned, her attention focused on Edward.

"You just told a lord to mind his manners!" Edward remonstrated, the words almost strangled from him. His eyes were wide, his face bright scarlet. "And not just any lord— *Viscount Chalmsy!*"

"Well, and so he must," Miss Carrington returned, speaking as if the viscount weren't lying there at her feet, perfectly able to hear every word she said. "It is growing darker by the minute, and we must get everyone back to the house and warmed and fed and the children to bed, and a doctor for his lordship's injuries, and we can't do that standing here listening to someone talk nonsense—not even if that someone

is a viscount. Besides, it feels as if it once again is coming
on to rain."

"*Julia*!" Jack thought poor Edward would drop from em-
barrassment, and smiled at the young man to ease his discomfiture.

"Perhaps you could find me a stick I could use as a
crutch," Jack suggested, speaking strictly to Edward and ignoring Miss Carrington as she had earlier ignored him. Edward turned eagerly to fulfill that request, but his sister
stopped him with a hand on his shoulder.

"There's nought that will bear his weight anywhere near,
Edward," Miss Carrington said, "I've already looked." She
transferred her gaze from her brother to the viscount, and
frowned heavily at him.

"Now, my lord," Miss Carrington said, "it obviously is not
what you might like, but it is all we have. So if you will just
lean on Edward and me, we will get you out of this ditch and
up onto the road and into the wagon. You need never tell any
of your society friends about this, and we certainly shall not!"

If the speech was meant to hearten the viscount it did not.
He responded testily that he was not concerned with what
his friends would think—he never worried about what people thought. But he did not wish to be burdening a woman
with his weight *or* his worries, and he would very much appreciate it if they would once again look for a stout stick to
aid him.

Jack had meant what he said in a gentlemanly way, even
if it had perhaps come out more angrily than he meant it to
sound, so he was astonished when Miss Carrington, instead
of doing as he wished, laughed. And laughed.

"Viscount Chalmsy," the lady said, straightening her lips
with an effort as she saw his look of amazement turn to one

of temper, "I have carried far bigger burdens, believe me! Now, please—I wished to get the children home. I can see William shivering despite his best efforts not to let me do so. And Lily will be coughing tomorrow for sure, if she remains much longer in the damp night air—to say nothing of the effect your time on the ground may have had on your own health. Please. No more nonsense. Edward?"

The young man seemed to know what she required, for Jack, still protesting, found himself on his feet in spite of himself, one arm draped around Edward's shoulder and the other wrapped around Miss Carrington. She had her hands at his waist, and tightened her hold as Jack tried to put weight on his injured leg and almost fell.

"That will not do, my lord," Miss Carrington chided him, her voice kind but firm. "You must let us carry you more than you like. Tell me, do you think you could hop on your good leg, since your hurt leg will not bear you?"

"Well, of course I can hop," Jack said, his voice growing more testy with each word. Viscount Chalmsy did not like relying on others, especially when the others were managing females. "But there is no need, I assure you. Just a step or two and then—"

He tried again to place weight on his bad ankle, and this time the effort took him to his knees. As he went down he brought his bearers down with him.

"Well, of all the pigheaded—" Miss Carrington began, then compressed her lips tightly together as she perceived the pleading look on her brother's face.

She counted to ten twice and then, when she thought she could speak in an even tone, the lady said, "Another step or two, my lord, and you will have us all in the basket for sure. Please. Let us help you. Hop on your good leg, and leave the role of hero for another time. When you are with someone else, who is impressed by such things."

"Julia!" Once more young Edward tried to remonstrate with his sister. "You can't talk to Viscount Chalmsy as if he were William's age!"

"Well, when he stops acting as if he is William's age, then I'll stop talking to him that way," Miss Carrington replied, her exasperation evident as she once again spoke as if the viscount were not there. "Until then—"

All the time they'd been talking the Carringtons had been acting, and Jack found himself again standing on his good leg, his bad one held off the ground with an effort he found quite wearing. With a glare bordering on dislike he said, through gritted teeth, "I am ready, Miss Carrington."

"As are we, my lord," the lady responded promptly, not at all put off by his baleful stare. In fact, she seemed not to notice it, which only increased Jack's temper. "Now. Hop!"

Despite what he might like, hop the viscount did, all the way out of the steep ditch, each step jarring his head and injured ankle, and all the other muscles and bones that were starting to protest their part in the accident. When they reached the top of the incline Miss Carrington told him, in a voice that did not brook argument, that he must put all his weight on her while Edward went to bring the wagon to them.

Since the wagon waited no more than twenty feet from where they stood, that order surprised Edward, who started to suggest that they could walk it as easily as not. He was stopped by his sister's offhand comment that she rather thought the viscount had covered enough distance for the night.

Jack, who minutes earlier had caviled at accepting the woman's help, could only lean gratefully on her, breathing heavily as he mentally blessed her for realizing he was spent.

It was Miss Carrington who positioned the viscount so that he could lift himself into the wagon with the least strain on his injured leg, and it was Miss Carrington who swung that leg into the wagon and called on Cressida to come take the viscount's ankle into her lap and keep it from bumping about during the journey home.

"Here, I say," Jack protested, not wanting his boot to dirty the young woman's dress. Miss Carrington overrode his concern with the prosaic statement that it was an old dress of Cressida's after all, and Julia herself could not see to him because she must lead his team while Edward drove the wagon.

Jack's weak suggestion that perhaps he could drive the wagon and Edward could hold his foot was met with a laugh and the admonishment not to be a fool. How, Miss Carrington asked him, could he hold the reins, when he could barely hold his head up?

Jack realized the fairness of her question, but he did not like to be called a fool any more than the next man, so he turned his head away and ignored her. His feelings were somewhat soothed when the younger Miss Carrington assured him that she would like above all things to be useful, and to spare him any pain she could, and when the two youngest Carringtons, upon being lifted into the wagon by their oldest sister and Edward, offered solemnly to each hold a hand, if that would make him feel better. Jack declined their offer, but told them he thought it most handsome, earning himself three Carrington smiles from their wagon's other occupants.

Tightening his jaw, the viscount awaited the inevitable

jolting he knew would occur in what he very accurately judged to be no more than a farm cart. He tried to position himself so that any knocks he took against the rough wood would, at least, fall on the uninjured side of his head. He was gritting his teeth, determined to bear it, when he felt a hand on his shoulder and looked up to see the eldest Miss Carrington once again nearby, holding something soft in her hands.

"For your head," the lady said, and placed what it took him several moments to realize was her shawl behind him. It smelled faintly of lavender, and for some ridiculous reason seemed to comfort him even as he protested.

"But you'll need—" he stated.

Miss Carrington gave him a brief smile.

"Not as much as you, my lord," the lady said, and vanished again. Edward gave the rawboned horse hitched to the wagon the office to start, and Jack, gazing toward the sky in tight-lipped concentration, tried to count raindrops to take his mind off the pain.

There were only a few at the time, for which Julia, watching the sky and trying to gauge when the clouds might open up again, was devoutly grateful. The few were all Jack needed, however, for the small train of Carringtons and their accidental guest had gone only one quarter of a mile when a particularly large rut in the road sent the viscount into his own private darkness again.

Chapter
Three

When Jack next awoke, daylight was streaming through the windows of a warm and pleasant room that was totally foreign to him. Lace curtains, old but well washed and starched, hung at the windows; an oak chest stood against the sloping wall to his left, and he lay in a matching oak four-poster bed with a soft down coverlet. But what he was doing there . . .

The viscount closed his eyes and frowned, trying to remember. The action made him wince. His head felt as if it were twice its regular size, and when he put a hand to it he began to think it was.

A soft "Oh, no!" made Jack opened his eyes, seeking the sound's source, and all that had happened returned to his memory as he once again found himself staring into the face of an angel. She was dressed in a simple gown of white cambric, trimmed with salmon ribbons, and the salmon ribbon threaded through her golden hair only contributed to her heavenly appearance.

"Oh, no, sir!" Cressida Carrington repeated, face and voice earnest. "You must not. The doctor has bandaged your head and you must not move the bandage. Really, you mustn't!"

"Bandaged—" Jack said, realizing as he said the word that that was why his head felt so big. "For a bump—"

24

Cressida nodded, smiling; it was obvious that she saw no reason that one bump should not elicit such care. Jack gazed toward the window, registering the sunlight in his mind, and asked if it was morning, then.

"Oh, no, my lord," Cressida told him, smiling a gentle smile Jack was sure Renaissance artists once painted—or should have. "It is nearly four o'clock. In the afternoon!"

"Afternoon—" Jack repeated the word blankly, then sat bolt upright, an unwise action that made him groan and sink back onto the pillows again. "It can't be!"

"But it is," the younger Miss Carrington assured him. "And you are not to move about like that! The doctor said you are to lie quite still, and not make any sudden movements or thrash about in any way! And *Julia* said so, too!"

It was obvious to Jack that Julia's word carried much more weight with Cressida than did the doctor's, and he smiled in spite of himself. That action was met by another smile from Cressida Carrington, and they sat smiling at each other for several moments before Jack roused himself to say, "But surely you have not sat up with me since I arrived here!"

He was both relieved and, in some recess of his mind, a little disappointed at her immediate disclaimer. This was accompanied by another smile and the information that it was Julia who had not left his side all through the night and until just perhaps two minutes before he awoke.

"I am to sit with you for five minutes while Julia goes and tells William he must not on any account put the garden snake in the vicar's hat," Cressida finished.

"He must not put the garden snake . . ." Jack tried to puzzle that out, wondering if the bump on his head was more serious than he had thought, because it made no sense to him.

He gave up trying to decipher the statement and asked instead why William would do such a thing.

"Because he wishes to," Cressida replied. Her bright eyes and cheerful smile made it apparent she believed her answer made all the sense in the world.

"He wishes—" Jack closed his eyes, shook his head slightly trying to clear it, and earned only a pang of pain for his trouble. He opened his eyes, and tried again.

"Why," the viscount asked, "would he wish to do such a thing?"

Cressida sighed. "William is very provoked," she explained. "The vicar—" She looked down at her hands and studied first their backs, then their fronts. It was clear she was working hard to find the appropriate words. "The vicar is something of a . . . of a . . . "

Jack grinned at her conscious efforts to be kind. "Pompous fellow, is he?"

Cressida nodded gratefully, and again her smile grew. "But Julia says that however tiresome the vicar may be, that is no excuse for William to put a snake in his hat, because you can't go around putting a snake in every tiresome person's hat, because Julia doubts there are that many snakes in all of England, and besides—"

Cressida looked up inquiringly at Jack's crack of laughter, but before she could ask just what the viscount found so amusing the door to the bedroom opened and Julia Carrington stepped inside.

The woman looked tired, Jack noted; there were shadows under her eyes, her shoulders slumped slightly, and several strands of hair had come loose from the neat knot at the nape of her neck. The hair curled around her face, softening her appearance. When the lady saw Jack awake she straightened her shoulders and said with a smile that seemed as relieved as it was genuine, "So you've decided to rejoin us, have you?"

Miss Carrington moved toward the bed to put a hand consideringly on the viscount's forehead. Whatever she felt there seemed to satisfy her, for she removed her hand and walked to a small table near the door; Jack frowned at the sight of the ominous brown bottle sitting there.

Miss Carrington picked up the bottle and a spoon and returned to the viscount, saying in her best dealing-with-a-sick-child voice, "Dr. Smythley left this for you; it's for your head, which I imagine must be aching dreadfully, yes?"

Jack hunched a shoulder and said it hurt some, but not enough to be taking some foul-tasting medicine he had no doubt would do him no good, anyway.

Miss Carrington smiled and poured some of the dark brown liquid into the spoon. When she held it out to him Jack frowned heavily up at her and clamped his lips together. Miss Carrington's smile grew.

"You are as bad as Edward and William," she told him, "but they at least have the excuse of being children—oh, dear! Please do not tell Edward I said that! He is very conscious of his age, and would be out of sorts with me for days if he knew I just placed him with William! And indeed I must not, for he is a young man now, and not a boy. He is forever telling me I must remember that, and of course he is right!"

Jack looked up at her, suspicious as she rattled on. He had an inkling that her conversation was a diversion, and his inkling was confirmed as the spoon grew nearer and nearer his mouth as the lady talked. When it was no more than two inches from his nose Miss Carrington said, in a heartening tone he was sure she often used with William and Lily, "Now, come, sir—this will help ease the pain, and surely you want that?"

Jack continued to glare, and Miss Carrington shook her head. The way she bit her lip as she took a step back made Jack think he'd won. He relaxed slightly and was just starting to smile when a decided gleam appeared in the lady's eye. His own eyes sharpened with suspicion, then he heard the lady say, "Cressida, would you give Viscount Chalmsy his medicine, please?"

The younger Miss Carrington rose and came gracefully forward, saying that she would be honored to do so, and she did hope it would not taste too terribly bad, because not for the world would she wish to force something horrid on the viscount, but it was for his own good, after all, and if he swallowed it right down, well, perhaps it wouldn't be so very awful, and she was sure Viscount Chalmsy was quite brave, really, although he wasn't appearing so at the moment, but he musn't mind that, because she wouldn't tell anyone and neither would Julia, and Cressida would understand if he couldn't bring himself to the sticking point . . . .

The words seemed to come on one breath, all soft and sympathetic, and after directing a fulminating eye toward Julia Carrington, the viscount opened his mouth and gulped the nasty stuff as the best cure for Cressida's artless chatter.

"There, now!" Cressida approved, beaming down at Jack. Her blue eyes shone with happiness. "I knew you would be terribly brave."

"Yes," said Cressida's older sister, her lips prim, her own eyes alight. "There, now!"

The viscount, put forcibly in mind of his sister-in-law by the expression on the eldest Miss Carrington's face, sneezed and closed his eyes. Fervently he prayed that heaven would deliver him from managing, sure-to-get-their-own-way women like Arabella, and Julia Carrington.

The next time Jack woke the room was almost in darkness; a fire burned quietly in the fireplace and Miss Carrington sat next to it, mending by the light of a single candle. As Jack watched she put a hand to her forehead and rubbed it wearily, then laid down her mending and rose. She stretched several times before she bent to stir something heating on the grate.

"What time is it?" Jack asked, the words coming out abrupt and louder than he had intended in the stillness. The lady turned to look at him in surprise.

"You're awake!" she said, moving toward the bed and ignoring his question. Once again Jack was submitted to the touch of her hand on his forehead; it felt gentle and cool, and he liked the feeling almost as much as he resented it.

"I'm not a child, you know!" he said, moving his head restlessly away from her.

She smiled. "I imagine we all feel rather childlike, when we are ill," she told him.

"Yes, well—" Jack frowned heavily. "Some people, perhaps." He tossed his head back and forth several times but could not get comfortable, not even when Miss Carrington turned the pillow for him, and plumped it several times.

"It's this bandage," the viscount said, ripping at it in frustration. "I can't lay my head down right when it's wrapped up to be twice its size."

In a moment he had the bandage off, and Miss Carrington shook her head reprovingly at him.

"Whoever heard of putting such a bandage on a small bump?" the viscount said in disgust.

The lady smiled in spite of herself, and her eyes danced. They were nice eyes, Jack decided; warm and humorous and kind.

"I must confess," Miss Carrington told him, "I wondered the same thing. But I am afraid your bump was a bit more serious than I thought—although you are doing quite well, and if you take your medicine you no doubt will be feeling much better in a few days."

Jack's grimace at the mention of medicine made her smile grow, and she sat down on the bed beside him to gently probe the bump on his forehead. The viscount sneezed.

"The truth is," Miss Carrington confided, "—God bless you!—I think it had never before come in Dr. Smythley's way to bandage a viscount's head, and he was rather taken with the prospect. I don't think it will hurt you to leave the bandage off, if you like, although the doctor won't like it, and I'm sure Cressida and Lily will be most disappointed when next they see you."

"They will?"

Jack stared at her in fascination, watching the way the firelight seemed to catch red highlights in her hair as he waited to hear why. He liked the way she moved—quietly, yet with such purpose. The confidence with which she went about the room made him feel cared for, and it occurred to Jack that if he was going to fall into a woman's hands because of an accident, he could do much worse than the competent hands of the calm and caring Miss Carrington—

The viscount caught himself up sharply, frowning at the thought. It was ridiculous, he decided, for the competent

Miss Carrington was also obviously bossy and managing, and she had laughed at him. Several times.

Jack did not like to be bossed, managed, or laughed at.

Perhaps, the viscount decided, gazing toward the fire, he really *did* have a fever after all, and that was why nothing made any sense—snakes in hats, and now this. Or perhaps he was dreaming it all.

At that thought Viscount Chalmsy brightened and tried to sit up; the pain the movement caused him made it clear he was awake, and he sank back into the bed with a loud sigh.

Miss Carrington, watching their guest curiously, waited until he was lying quietly before continuing their conversation.

"Cressy and Lily thought your bandage most romantic," she told him. "I fear a bandaged foot is not nearly as good. Nor the sniffles you seem to be developing." She considered a moment before adding that she doubted there was anything more unromantic than sniffles—unless it was the influenza.

Jack, not wanting to debate the merits of sniffles and influenza in the romance department, sneezed again, then looked at her in amazement.

"Miss Carrington," he demanded, "are you laughing at me again? A bandaged head romantic! Indeed!"

Julia shook her head. "Oh, no, sir," she assured him, her eyes wide even as a distinct tremor sounded in her voice. "I am not laughing at you. Although I might have to grin a little at the silliness of it all."

Jack's gaze was suspicious. "All?"

"Life!"

"Oh." Jack quirked an eyebrow, then lowered it because of the pang his head suffered for the effort. He gazed at her for several moments, gauging the sincerity of her answer before he asked, puzzled, "Do you often laugh at life, Miss Carrington?"

"Oh, often!" she assured him with a smile. "It seems only fair, I think, since I often have the distinct impression that life is laughing at me! And surely it is better to laugh than to cry, don't you agree?"

The lady had risen as she spoke and was moving toward the table that held the ominous brown bottle. Jack was imperious as he told her she might as well stop right there, because he wasn't taking that blasted stuff again, no matter what. Julia turned and eyed him.

"I'm not!" Jack raised his chin and frowned, looking as pugnacious as a man can who has a bump on his head and is tied to his bed by an injured ankle and many other hurts and bruises.

The lady shrugged.

"Then perhaps you would take the broth I've been keeping warm for you," Miss Carrington said, and switched directions. She walked toward the grate and returned a moment later with a cup of steaming liquid.

"Broth?" Jack wrinkled his nose in distaste. Miss Carrington grinned.

"It will be very good for your sniffles," she told him. "And tomorrow, if you are very good, and there is no sign of fever, the doctor says you may have a piece of baked chicken."

"I would rather have a pint of ale and a good sirloin!" Jack protested. Miss Carrington looked at him. It was the look, he was sure, that often brought William—and probably Edward, too—into hasty compliance with their sister's will.

"I think not, sir," Miss Carrington said, handing him the

cup. Jack sipped in silence for several moments, at first sulky and then surprised to find he enjoyed the contents much more than he cared to admit—or would. He eyed the lady consideringly.

"You never did answer my question," the viscount said abruptly. Miss Carrington looked at him in surprise.

"Question?"

"I asked what time it is."

Miss Carrington shrugged. "Shortly after midnight, I would think."

Jack choked on the broth. *"What?"*

Miss Carrington dabbed with her handkerchief at where he had dribbled broth, wiping his chin as if he were William or Lily as she repeated, her voice calm, "Shortly after midnight, I think. I believe I heard the clock in the hallway chime not too long ago."

"My good woman," Jack said, struggling to sit up straighter and finding his efforts frustrated by Miss Carrington, who pushed him firmly back again, "whatever are you doing sitting up with me at this hour?"

Julia appeared surprised. "Well, someone has to—" she started.

"I believe your sister told me you sat up with me through the *last* night," Jack said, frowning. "Surely you have not been here all this time. And you are wrong—*no one* has to; there is not the least need!"

"I lay down upon my bed for nearly an hour before supper and Edward sat with you," the lady soothed, tipping the cup of broth toward his lips again. She ignored his last statement and watched him as he drank the broth almost absently as he glared at her. "And now that you've awakened and had your supper, when Edward comes at two to relieve me, he will sit with you through the rest of the night—"

"An *hour*?" Jack repeated, cutting her off. "You lay down for *an hour*? Miss Carrington, really! I do not require such devotion, I assure you! I am not used to it, I do not want it, and I repeat, there is no reason for it. There is no reason for you to sit up with me, or for Edward to do so."

Miss Carrington took the now-empty cup from him and placed it on the table. She toyed with the items there for several minutes, her back to him, and a sixth sense told the viscount that she was struggling with herself. Struggling mightily, even as she turned back toward him.

"I see," Miss Carrington said, her face devoid of expression, her words coming out careful and soft. "You are, of course, perfectly able to take care of yourself."

"Yes," Jack said. "I am—"

"Unless, of course, you need anything," the lady continued, cutting him off as he had earlier done to her. Her words were coming faster now, and there was an edge to them. Belatedly Jack remembered the times out of mind his grandfather and brother had adjured him to think before he spoke.

"For with a bump on your head to make you dizzy, and sneezing we must hope won't turn to a cough and go to your lungs, and an ankle that doesn't work—you will be glad to hear, Viscount Chalmsy, that your ankle is not broken, although it is badly sprained, and Dr. Smythley says it will be some time before it is fully recovered . . . Where was I?" Miss Carrington stopped herself, and Jack realized her color was rising with her voice. He shifted uneasily. "Oh, yes! Fine people we would be, once you were injured through the actions of members of our family, if we simply left you to see to yourself as best you might so that we could sleep. Or perhaps we could just put you in your phaeton and slap the reins and see where your horses take you! It wouldn't be our worry, would it? Except of course we can't do that, because your team needs attention, too, and there is a wheel off your phaeton—"

Jack was staring, his jaw slightly agape and his own color heightened, when the lady stopped abruptly and pressed her hands to her cheeks. She took a deep breath and said, in a mortified tone, that she must beg his pardon; she was a bit more tired than she had thought, and she had not meant to speak so, for she was deeply sorry for his injury, and she realized that her family was completely responsible for it, and they would do everything they could to repair—to repair—

"Miss Carrington," Jack interrupted, mortified himself by her obvious discomfort, "I apologize."

Miss Carrington shook her head as if she had not heard correctly. Her face was puzzled as she stared at him. "You—?"

"I apologize," the viscount repeated. "You are perfectly right, of course; I'm lying here helpless as a babe, and I find I dislike that above all things. I have never before encountered it—not since I *was* a babe, anyway, and of course I don't remember that! I spoke without thinking—my brother and grandfather—my sister-in-law, I'm *sure*—would tell you it is a very bad habit of mine. I appreciate your concern. And it was not at all the fault of your family that I was injured; I was thinking of other things and took that corner faster than I should have on a road I was not familiar with."

"Well . . ."

Good manners prevented Miss Carrington from agreeing with him, and in spite of himself Jack grinned. What the lady did not say was writ on her face so plainly that there was no reason to give voice to it.

He let his grin grow, knowing it was the grin that caused female hearts to flutter in London, and almost always won him what he wanted. It was why he grinned just so.

"Miss Carrington," the viscount said, turning slightly so he could observe her more closely, "what would you say if I told you that you put me forcibly in mind of my sister-in-law, who, although I am most displeased with her at the moment and hold her personally responsible for all that has happened to me, and whose neck I would cheerfully wring were she to walk through that door at the moment and be so obliging as to render her neck up to me—which she is not at all! obliging, I mean—is still the most redoubtable woman I know, although she does not reach my shoulder in height, and looks as if a wind might blow her away?"

Miss Carrington's response to his compliment and grin was not what the viscount expected. She did not blush or stutter or looked pleased, or react in any other way like the women of his acquaintance.

Miss Carrington's expression was one of clear disbelief as she gazed down her regal nose and offered up a blunt reply.

"Stuff!" said Miss Carrington, resuming her seat by the fire and paying the viscount no more heed. It was only after Jack had closed his eyes and been quiet for several minutes that he heard, once again, a very low, "Stuff!"

When the viscount drifted off to sleep he was smiling. It was a smile that lasted all night, as Jack dreamed pleasant dreams.

Chapter Four

The next time Viscount Chalmsy awoke it was with a violent sneeze and the feeling that his throat was on fire. He opened his eyes to the soft gray light that presaged dawn as it filtered through the curtains of his room; when he turned his head he saw Edward Carrington asleep in the chair by the now-dying fire.

Jack watched the young man for several moments until another sneeze overtook him. As the sound echoed in the room Edward roused and shook himself, jumping from the chair to add another log to the fire and to vigorously stir the ashes burning there. After applying the poker with more enthusiasm than expertise, Edward turned and met the viscount's eyes. The younger man flushed guiltily as he asked, with some hesitancy, "Have you been awake long, my lord? I hope I wasn't too noisy just now."

The viscount sneezed.

"No, no," Jack said in a gravelly voice that made him frown when he heard it. "I had awakened just shortly before you did."

"Oh!" Edward flushed further, and came toward the bed, saying shamefacedly, "I shouldn't have dozed off like that, I know. Jules would have my head for washing if she knew."

The unspoken plea behind the words made the viscount promise at once that he would tell no one of what Edward obviously regarded as a lapse in responsibility. Jack added handsomely that he really didn't see why anyone else should stay awake when he himself was sleeping so soundly.

"Well, that's rather what I thought," Edward agreed, leaning forward and lowering his voice as if confessing to a great conspiracy. "But Julia said you might waken and if you did you might need something, and we should see that you are as comfortable as we can make you, you being our guest. I suggested you might just shout if you wanted something, but Jules gave me one of her looks and said she rather doubted you would do that, and I suppose she's right, really. I don't suppose it's something a lord would do, is it?"

Viscount Chalmsy, who had no trouble thinking of any number of lords he believed would shout right out anytime they wanted anything, forbore to speak for all the aristocracy. He said instead that he himself would not like to disrupt a household by shouting, then added ruefully that the way his voice sounded, he probably wouldn't be heard, anyway.

"Yes, well . . . " Edward nodded, looking down. Then he sighed. "Jules was right again. She usually is."

Jack grinned, the young man's woeful expression taking the viscount's mind from his own troubles for the moment. "Disgustingly so, I take it?"

Edward glanced up, startled, then met Jack's grin with a bashful one of his own. "Please don't misunderstand me, my lord," he said. "Jules is a great gun—the best! Well, she has had to be, hasn't she? But sometimes . . . "

He paused when he noticed the slight frown on the viscount's forehead, and looked at Jack questioningly. He did not have to wait to hear what puzzled the viscount.

"Excuse me," Jack said, rubbing his forehead slightly and wiping away the sweat that had gathered there. "I seem to be confused; sometimes I think your sister's name is Julia, and other times I swear I hear you say Jules; unless my hearing—"

Edward made haste to assure Viscount Chalmsy that it wasn't his hearing. The young man was rather abashed as he explained that he and his brothers and sisters often called their eldest sister Jules as a nickname.

"When William was a baby Papa was always calling Julia his little jewel, and when William said it, it always came out 'Jules,' so Jules she has been ever since to us," Edward said. "I don't suppose it sounds very ladylike, does it?"

"When I first heard it, I thought the name must belong to a man," the viscount said, rubbing his forehead again.

"Oh?" Edward thought about that for a moment, then agreed that it might be true. "And if Julia were a man, I'm sure she'd be with Wellington now, serving as his right arm."

Something in the young man's face suggested to the viscount that Miss Carrington often had the ordering of her brother's life much more than was to Edward's liking, and Jack nodded in sympathy as he gave another sneeze.

"A born commander, is she?" the viscount said. "I thought so when I met her. And I know just what you mean. I have a sister-in-law much like her—bossy and interfering and all the time saying they only have your best interests at heart, which is usually true, plague take them!"

"Yes!" Edward's grin grew. "But I don't suppose a sister-in-law is as bad as a sister, because surely your sister-in-law cannot interfere in your life as much—"

"She can interfere enough," Jack interjected, with sufficient feeling to make his young host pause.

"Oh? Well." Edward tried to think of something comforting to say. "But at least if your sister-in-law bothers you badly enough, you can go away."

"My dear, boy," Jack said, the words coming out almost as dry as his throat, "that is exactly what landed me in this imbroglio!"

"Oh!" A surprised Edward waited for more. When it did not come, manners prevented him from pressing the viscount; instead, he changed the subject to say Julia had told him that when their guest next awoke Edward was to see if there was anything he could help Viscount Chalmsy with. It was an offer the viscount gratefully accepted.

Jack had just finished shaving, with young Edward's willing if inexpert aid, and with no more than half a basin of water dumped on him as Edward strove to provide assistance in the viscount's morning grooming, when there was a light rap on the door.

Viscount Chalmsy was feeling more than a little worn after attending to his morning exigencies; he felt as if he had been pummeled from head to toe by the great Gentleman Jackson himself, and it had been a struggle to hold his temper and caustic tongue while receiving the tender ministrations of his young attendant. Holding his temper and tongue was not an exercise the viscount normally engaged in, but for some reason, looking at Edward's eager face and finding the young man so ready to please, Jack discovered he did not wish to hurt the fellow's feelings.

Perhaps it was this miserable cold, the viscount thought glumly—it took the will to wound right out of him. Jack tried to imagine what his valet would say of such untoward behavior, and wondered if perhaps he should put it down to the bump on his head.

Still, Jack did not know how much longer he could keep to his resolve not to snap at his host, for Edward was proving to be one of those infernal people who talked cheerfully and nonstop in the morning. The viscount, a born night owl, had long made it known to his compatriots that he was of the opinion that in a truly civilized world, no conversation would be exchanged before nine o'clock in the morning, and nothing of any true import would occur until well after noon. He was clamping his jaws together and wondering how in the world to get young Carrington to leave him alone when a light knock was followed by the door opening.

Julia Carrington entered the room, carrying a tray. She was dressed in a simple gown of warm rose that set off her chestnut hair, and Jack relaxed slightly at the sight of her.

Miss Carrington seemed to take in the situation at a glance, for after looking at the viscount's face and then at her brother, who was replacing the viscount's shaving gear in the rather bedraggled portmanteau the Carringtons had rescued from the ditch Jack's accident had pitched him into, she said pleasantly, "Edward, dear, I've brought the viscount his breakfast, so you can just pop down now and have your own. And after that, would you check the poultice on the gray's hock? I've changed it once, and it may need changing again; you'll know."

Edward nodded and said that he'd be quite happy to do so, although if his lordship wished, he'd be happy to stay and visit with him a bit more, too. Jack responded with more force than tact that no, no, he would not want to keep Edward from his breakfast or his work. When he uttered a vio-

lent sneeze the viscount seized upon that as an excuse for
Edward to stay away from him; in fact, he suggested, they
should *all* stay away from him, to avoid contracting his infernal cold.

Seeing the amused expression on Miss Carrington's face,
and experiencing the uneasy feeling that the lady might be
reading his mind, the viscount amended his thought silently
to hope that if anyone contracted his infernal cold it would
be Miss Carrington, because he could not help but feel that
that would serve her right. Aloud he added that he would
much appreciate Edward checking his team, for the viscount
would never forgive himself if they'd come to lasting harm
through his own carelessness.

Edward agreed at once to see to the horses, and hurried
off to do so. As soon as he left the room Miss Carrington settled the large tray she carried across the viscount's lap, and
remarked comfortably that he need not worry about his
horses; they would take no lasting harm.

Jack gave a noncommittal grunt and eyed with disfavor
the dry toast and tea before him. Miss Carrington smiled and
said, as she tucked a snowy linen napkin under his chin, "I
am thinking, my lord, that you are one of those people who
do not wish for conversation first thing in the morning."

A brief "Quite so" was followed by several moments of
silence. At last the viscount, disgruntled, poked at the toast
and sneezed upon it before looking up at Miss Carrington,
his eyes filled with frown. "What *is* this, anyway?"

"Why," the lady said, her eyebrows raised in surprise, "it
is your breakfast, of course!"

"It is no breakfast of mine!" Jack returned. His eyes narrowed as her widened, for Jack had a very good idea that

that look of innocence was playacting, not real. "Toast and tea indeed! Take it away and bring me something fit to eat!"

He sneezed again.

A reasonable Miss Carrington said that what was before him was most fit to eat—especially for an invalid. She placed a cool hand on his forehead, and Jack felt unreasonably bereft when she removed it.

The lady seemed to consider for a moment, and he saw her glance toward the doctor's brown bottle before she continued her conversation, noting that she had breakfasted on toast and tea herself that morning, as well as a morsel of ham, and some eggs.

"Ham!" Jack repeated. His face brightened even as his eyes watered. "Eggs! Yes. That will do! Take this away at once, and bring me that!"

Miss Carrington shook her head, and Jack's heavy frown descended again.

"You forget, Viscount Chalmsy," Miss Carrington said firmly, "that you are injured. And you have a fever."

"And you, Miss Carrington, forget who I am!"

The viscount snapped the words, then turned deep red, aghast that such a gauche statement had come from his mouth. He wished that the bed would swallow him up almost as sincerely as he hoped it was the fever speaking. Never before had the viscount referred to his rank or privilege vocally. It did not console him to realize, upon reflection, that never before had he had any reason to do so.

Viscount Chalmsy, the future earl of Clangstone, had always had his position recognized and assured for him. For years he had been cosseted and bowed and scraped to because of it. Now here he lay, like some encroaching mushroom, his throat tickling, his nose running, his eyes watering, and sounding as if he were trying to puff off his consequence for eggs and ham.

Jack cursed himself not just for uttering the words, but for saying them to someone in Miss Carrington's position. It occurred to him too late that he probably had humiliated the woman beyond bearing, for the way she was dressed and the clean but slightly shabby state of his room suggested to him that the Carringtons lived modestly. Jack knew that the addition of one of London's leaders to their household must be a strain. He would have to apologize, and since Jack hated above all things to have to apologize . . .

All this went through his mind, only to be immediately erased by Miss Carrington's reaction.

Miss Carrington, far from being humiliated by his snappish reply, crinkled up her nose, giggled, then laughed.

And laughed.

And laughed.

"I am glad, Miss Carrington, to afford you such amusement," Jack said. Hostility dripped from every word, and Miss Carrington laughed again.

"No, my lord, you are not," she assured him. "No doubt you'd like nothing more than to put your fingers around my neck and wring some sense into me, but believe me, I shall keep my neck far from your reach! And you are wrong when you say I forget who you are! I know that very well! You are Viscount Chalmsy, a leader of the ton, which I don't care about at all although the thought has Edward and the rest of the children in awe. You are also a guest in our home, which I care about very much. You will *be* our guest while you mend the injuries sustained in part by the actions of members of my family, and while you recover from this raging head cold that no doubt makes you short-tempered—although I would imagine patience is not your long suit at the best of times, especially when you are not getting your way.

"You are an invalid—much spoiled, I would guess, for this strong tendency of yours to revert to the tantrums of a five-year-old each time your will is thwarted gives you away. You are another mouth to feed and more work than either our servants or we need, and for that reason I would like to see you well and on your way as quickly as possible—not, of course, that I don't want you well for your own sake, which I most certainly do—and for that reason I intend to follow the doctor's orders. Tea and toast this morning, sir. Perhaps, if there is no fever tomorrow, a little egg then. Perhaps."

Jack, who was glaring at her, thought Edward had underestimated the woman when he said she would be with Wellington were she a man. Jack thought she might very well be *commanding* Wellington.

For several moments the viscount stared at her, then he said in a stiff if thready voice that showed just how affronted he really was that he had no wish to be a burden to her or her household, and that he would be happy to remove to the nearest inn that very morning. Miss Carrington laughed again.

"Oh, please, my lord," she said, putting her hand to his forehead and keeping it there, despite his impatient tossing of his head. "Do not poker up on me, for I haven't the time for it! For one thing, you are in no condition to even consider moving for several days. I should imagine you feel as if you've been trampled by horses, and you must be very much wishing that I will go away and leave you alone so that you can lie still and sleep as much as you can for as long as you can—something I will do as soon as you eat your breakfast. And in any case, there is no inn nearby that would be up to your expectations."

She removed her hand, and Jack looked at her strangely. "You have a very poor opinion of me, don't you, Miss Carrington?" he asked.

Viscount Chalmsy did not often encounter women who held him in low esteem.

The lady smiled, and shook her head, disclaiming. "I have no opinion of you at all, my lord," she said. "That would be impertinent of me, and I hope I am not guilty of impertinence, in addition to all the other social sins you must now be laying at my door. But I *do* know who you *are*, Viscount Chalmsy."

Jack, torn between the ungentlemanly desire to tell her that he didn't believe she cared a whit about being thought impertinent—indeed, he believed impertinence must be her middle name—and an uneasiness engendered by the unsettling feeling that her large brown eyes saw much more than many people's, had the fanciful notion that what she said was true; that she did know him, perhaps better than he would like. It was not a thought that pleased him, and he hoped it was the fever that put it into his head. He glared up at her for a moment before saying, in quite his stiffest voice, "Would it be too much to hope, then, that if I am to eat this infernal toast, I might at least have a little jam?"

It was not too much to ask; Miss Carrington disappeared and returned within a few minutes, carrying what might possibly have been the best strawberry jam Jack had ever tasted. Smearing it liberally on the now-cold toast, he ate in silence, scorning the tea despite—or because of—Miss Carrington's assertions that he would find it quite medicinal. His sotto voce assertion that he would find ale even more restorative was met with tranquil silence, and the viscount decided that if the lady could ignore him in that way, then he could ignore her, as well. Which he did, staring pointedly toward the window as he ate, only watching out of the corner of his eye the way she reached for her sewing basket, which she'd left the night before by the chair next to the fire, and quietly began to mend a small shirt he assumed belonged to William. The shirt had been patched before, he could see, and without thinking he fingered the fine linen of his own nightshirt.

Finally he turned to glare at Miss Carrington, still fingering his nightshirt. A horrifying thought occurred to him and he sat bolt upright, heedless of his head and ankle and all the other muscles that protested violently at that sudden movement. His quick action set him to coughing and sent his tray off his lap, spilling tea onto the worn rug beside the bed.

"Oh!" Jack said, grabbing too late for the cup. Miss Carrington was beside him in an instant, but her attention was not directed toward the tea, as he would have expected; her full attention rested on him.

"My lord!" she said, her eyes anxious. "Are you all right? Is there something amiss?"

Jack, touched by her evident concern, flushed slightly and said that he was fine; what was amiss was that he'd spilled tea on her rug, and he was quite sorry.

Miss Carrington, thus assured, turned her attention to the rug, scrubbing vigorously at the tea stain with the napkin that had been on Jack's tray. Several times she crossed to the water basin to wet the cloth and bring it back to scrub again. While she worked she assured him that it was of no moment; that accidents happened, as he was very well aware. She was kneeling on the floor as she spoke, and Jack watched as she piled the pieces of the broken teacup and plate onto the tray she'd retrieved from where it had slipped to the foot of the bed. Then she rose.

"I'll just take these down to the kitchen," she began, but Jack stayed her by the simple expedient of reaching out his hand and grasping her wrist.

"Miss Carrington—" he began, then seemed at a loss as to how to proceed. When he coughed her eyes once again grew anxious.

"Viscount Chalmsy," she said, "*are* you all right? Please, do not try to be brave with me, for if there is anything wrong I will have the doctor sent for at once."

Jack shook his head, then closed his eyes at the pain that caused. Miss Carrington, shifting the tray to her right arm, used the left hand Jack still held to push him gently back against the pillows.

"Really, sir, you must rest," she told him, her voice kind.

Jack opened his eyes again and said, without preamble, "Miss Carrington, I am wearing my nightshirt."

The lady, who knew that, nodded. "We found it in your portmanteau, and thought you would be more comfortable—"

Jack brushed that explanation aside with an impatient wave of his hand. "Yes, yes," he said. "Of course you were right! But the thing is—"

He stopped and Miss Carrington, not comprehending, waited.

"The thing is—" Jack started again, stopped, and in spite of himself felt his cheeks grow warm. He hoped Miss Carrington would put that down to fever, and applied his handkerchief to his nose.

Slowly Julia began to comprehend his anxiety; she bit her lip and tilted her head downward so the viscount could not see the sparkle growing in her eyes.

"I was wondering—" Jack tried, pausing again. Miss Carrington grinned as she took pity on him.

"Edward and our good Bosley put you into your nightshirt, my lord," she replied primly, "both seeming to feel you would be more comfortable with their help than with mine."

A relieved Jack said, "Well, thank goodness for that!" He realized too late that it was not the most felicitous of remarks, and looked up guiltily to add, "That is—"

Miss Carrington shook her head at him. "I know perfectly well what you mean, my lord," she said, "so there is no need for you to try to sugarcoat it now. Bosley is doing his best to redeem the coat you were wearing, but I am not sure—"

Jack dismissed his coat with a shrug, and Julia smiled. "I hope, my lord, that you feel the same way about your boots?"

Jack looked at her. "My boots?" he asked, and the pain in his voice had nothing to do with his injury. The boots he'd been wearing were his newest pair, especially fine. It was known in town that Viscount Chalmsy cared a great deal about good boots.

The lady nodded. "I had to cut your right one off. To relieve the swelling."

"You cut—" Jack repeated, stunned.

Miss Carrington nodded again. "Funny," she said, her head tilted to the side as she once again prepared to depart. "That is just what Edward said, when he returned yesterday after fetching the doctor!"

She wasn't sure, as she went out the door, if the stifled groan that followed her was due to his lordship's loss, or his lordship's shifting of his weight. Actually, it was due to his lordship picturing Phipps's face when the valet heard of this tragedy Viscount Chalmsy was sure his man would take most personally.

Chapter
Five

Jack slipped in and out of sleep the rest of the day. At one point in late morning he was awakened by a bluff individual Miss Carrington introduced as Dr. Smythley. The good doctor, after poking and prodding the viscount much more than Jack thought necessary—an opinion he acidly shared with the man of medicine, to Miss Carrington's amusement and the doctor's amazement—said that the patient was coming along as well as could be expected, and in a few days would find himself feeling much better if he just stayed in bed, took care of his cold and injuries, and followed the doctor's orders.

Jack's sulky rejoinder that he very much doubted that he would ever feel better only drew him a hearty pat on the shoulder from the doctor, and a quickly suppressed smile from Miss Carrington.

Recommending that Jack take his medicine and rest quietly, the doctor withdrew, oblivious to the pungent comments that followed his departure. Jack's assertion that he had been resting quietly when the doctor awakened him, and he did not appreciate that awakening, was followed by the declaration that he was on no account going to take any more of that nasty brown liquid Miss Carrington had forced

down his throat by her nefarious means the day before. Both
statements earned him no more than a quirked eyebrow
from the lady, and a recommendation not to work himself
into a pother over nothing.

The viscount was at once incensed at being accused of
working himself into a pother, when he was, as he said
loudly, only making conversation, should anyone care to listen to him—something, he added acidly, it appeared Miss
Carrington would not do! Besides, he told the room at large,
for he did not believe he was speaking to the lady, he was
never in a pother. Never.

Pulling the covers more closely around his shoulders, the
viscount turned his back to Miss Carrington who, after seeing the doctor out, had resumed her place by the fire. In seconds Jack was asleep again.

The next time Viscount Chalmsy opened his eyes it was
to find two small faces on a level with his own, regarding
him fixedly. Jack pulled back and blinked at them several
times, startled by their close proximity. William nodded in
satisfaction.

"See, Lily, I told you," the blond-headed boy said cheerfully. "He was only sleeping."

Lily appeared relieved and reached out to gently pat the
viscount's cheek. "You sleep with your mouth open, my
lord," she informed him. "But only just a little. And you
hardly drool at all!"

The little girl beamed at him as if she had just delivered a
piece of vital and welcome information. Jack, not knowing
what to say, was saved from having to say anything by the
soft click of an opening door. He had no question as to who
entered, even though he did not turn, because the children's
faces lit at sight of his newest visitor, and a quiet voice at

once said, "William! Lily! Come away from there before you wake the viscount!"

Lily's happy assurance that there was no need to come away, since his lordship was already awake, was met by a rueful, "Oh, dear!"

Moments later Miss Carrington appeared behind the children, once again holding a tray. Viscount Chalmsy frowned at her.

"If that is more toast and tea, Miss Carrington, you may take it away at once," Jack informed her. "I won't eat it!" Then he sneezed and swallowed, grimacing at the way his throat felt when he did so.

William and Lily appeared startled by the vehemence in the viscount's tone, and they glanced toward their sister for reassurance. It was clear to Jack that the children were amazed that anyone would speak to Julia Carrington in that way.

Their sister smiled reassuringly as she told the children, in a kind and forebearing voice that set the viscount's teeth on edge, that his lordship was feeling out of sorts because of his miserable head cold and injuries, so they must forgive and forget his rudeness and come back in a day or two, when he would be more thankful for the company.

Then, in a voice that practically dripped with tolerance, she said, as if to a small child, "There, there, my lord. You will feel better once you have eaten!"

The viscount, whose sometimes famous rudeness never before had been met straight on with a reference to it, forbore, until the children left the room, to say that there was some company he was not sure he would *ever* be thankful for, and that he wasn't at all sure he would ever feel better again, the way his head was splitting.

Miss Carrington said, "Handsome is as handsome does," —a reference he didn't understand but was quite sure was not a compliment—and prepared to set down the tray. Jack glanced at it suspiciously.

"Well?" he asked, glaring at the covered dishes as he tried to cough away the tickle in his scratchy throat. "I told you, if it's toast—"

The lady smiled and removed the first cover, displaying a bowl of chicken soup with chunks of vegetables dotting the broth. As the scent rose to Jack's nostrils he felt his mouth water, and he reached for the napkin laid to the side of the tray.

"I say!" he said. "That smells good! And I didn't think I'd be able to smell anything for days!"

Miss Carrington smiled again and removed the cover of the second dish, which contained a small serving of pudding. Jack, who normally loathed pudding, fell to with a will, and in no time had cleansed his plate, saying, when he was done, that he hoped she would present his compliments to the chef. Julia grinned.

"I told you you would feel better once you'd eaten," she said. The viscount frowned at her.

"Must you always be right, Miss Carrington?" he asked.

The question appeared to surprise her, for she tilted her head to the side, considering for several moments before she replied, "*Must* I? I don't think so. . . . Although I must say it is more comforting to be right than wrong, and I would much rather *be* right . . . ."

Jack, who hadn't meant to start a philosophical discussion, tried another question. "And do you do that on purpose, too?" he demanded.

The lady looked at him, her eyes questioning.

"Bait me," Jack said. "Oh, yes! You know you do!"

In the face of his insistence, she did not try to deny it. Instead, a twinkle appeared in her eye, and she said, "Alas, my lord, you have found me out!"

"Then you *do* do it on purpose!" Jack was astounded. He'd grown so used to being courted and praised and flattered and followed that he had little experience with baiting, having encountered it only on occasion from his sister-in-law, Arabella. Not even his brother, Charles, who stood in the best position to do so, had ever baited Jack much; probably, the viscount thought, because Charles did not have the disposition to do so. A sweet-tempered fellow, was Charles.

Jack, on the other hand—Jack himself was a *master* baiter . . . .

"I'm sure it is very bad of me," Miss Carrington said, curious to know the thoughts behind the expressions flitting across his face, but too polite to ask, "and I suppose I should apologize to you for it. One of my besetting sins always *has* been levity—the vicar has told me so times out of mind. But my lord!" She giggled in spite of herself. "You are so very *easy!*"

It took Jack a moment to assimilate her words, for the sound of her giggle had taken him aback. When Miss Carrington giggled she sounded like a much different person than the woman who seemed to be forever giving him orders and arguing with him; as if she were younger, somehow, and freer.

He let that thought go, however, as he realized what she'd said.

"*Easy*?" he demanded, his forehead wrinkling as he frowned. "What do you mean by that? Are you suggesting that I am *arrogant*, perhaps? Pompous? An ignorant coxcomb?"

The suggestion so obviously infuriated him that Julia giggled again.

"Not *ignorant*, my lord," she soothed, ignoring the way he obviously waited for her to refute "arrogant," "pompous," and "coxcomb," as well. As she watched his brows draw together it was all she could do not to laugh as she changed the subject with, "I thought you would like to know, Viscount Chalmsy, that we have sent word to your family of your accident."

Jack, far from appearing gratified at that news, frowned heavily even as he sneezed in her direction. "Why?" he demanded.

Miss Carrington blinked at him in surprise.

"Well, I am sure they would want to know!" she told him. "After all, if any of my family was injured, I would wish to know so that I might attend them, and make sure they had everything they need."

"Oh, yes!" Jack said. He reached absently for the tea Miss Carrington had set on his tray, and did not notice her quickly suppressed smile as he drained it. "I am sure you would! So you could descend upon them and bully them about while they were tied to their beds and unable to escape you! Which is just what Arabella will do, I'm sure, and I shall have to listen to who knows how many lectures on how this never would have occurred if I hadn't left London in that precipitous manner—"

"*Did* you leave London in a precipitous manner?" Miss Carrington asked, curious.

Jack frowned at her. "No! I did not! Just because a fellow doesn't wish to get himself leg shackled to some simpering miss—"

He stopped, aware that Miss Carrington, who had been approaching with the ominous brown bottle in hand, was eyeing him keenly. She even leaned slightly forward as if she all at once was deeply interested in what he had to say. As his conversation came to an abrupt halt she straightened and took a step forward, saying pleasantly, "Then you are not in favor of marriage, my lord?"

Jack waved an impatient hand—it was a gesture Miss Carrington was coming to recognize as one of his own—and raised a shoulder, to the shoulder's obvious discomfort. "Well," he said, "I suppose it is all right for some people, like Charles."

"Charles is your brother," Miss Carrington said.

Jack nodded. "But as for me—no. I am not in favor of marriage for me, Miss Carrington." He watched with a forbidding eye as she poured a measure of liquid in the brown bottle into the spoon she held, then said, "And if you think I am going to swallow that, you may think again, for I am not."

Miss Carrington looked down at the medicine, then up at the viscount, then down at the medicine again.

"I tell you what, my lord," she said, the words coming out slowly, as if she thought deeply about each before she said it. "I will make you a bargain."

"A bargain." The suspicion in Jack's voice made her look up and smile.

"A bargain," She nodded.

She had moved the spoon a little closer to his mouth, and

Jack moved back into the pillows, turning his head slightly as he asked, "And what is this bargain, pray?"

Miss Carrington smiled at him again. "My bargain is this, my lord," she said. "I will no longer drive you to distraction by pushing this medicine at you if you will not drive me to distraction by falling in love with my sister!"

"What?" Jack more yelped than said the word, and as he opened his mouth Miss Carrington quickly tilted the spoonful of liquid down it. Jack choked, swallowed, and glared balefully at her.

"I see how you keep your bargains!" he sputtered. The lady raised her eyebrows at him, and his temper rose.

"But we had not agreed, my lord," Miss Carrington said, her face tranquil. "You had not said yes! You had only said *'What?'* We had not shaken hands!"

"Yes, well—" Jack frowned at her, and said abruptly, "there are any number of anxious mamas, you know, who would be happy to the point of delirium should I fall madly in love with their darling daughters!"

Her obviously placating tone did everything but that as Miss Carrington said that she did not doubt it, but she was not an anxious mama, and she hoped he would be able to control his emotions when it came to Cressida.

"For," she told him candidly, "it seems so few men can, and it is such a nuisance, really, to have them moping about the house. All the young men in the district have at one time or another—and some of them still do. It is such a bother."

"Moping about?" Revolted by the picture that conjured in his mind, Jack told her in no uncertain terms that he did not *mope.* Nor, he said, did his taste run to young innocents, no matter how lovely they might be, and there was no denying

that Miss Carrington's sister was quite the loveliest young woman he had ever seen.

"Yes," Julia agreed, with enthusiasm. "She is quite beautiful, isn't she? And such a happy nature, too! If only—"

She stopped suddenly and said that she could see his lordship's eyelids growing heavy, and she did not wish to keep him awake with further conversation. She started to take the tray from his lap, but was stayed by his prompting. "If only?" Jack asked.

Miss Carrington smiled down at him, and it was clear that whatever she had been about to say would go unsaid.

"It is not your concern, my lord," the lady said, and Jack did not think it only his imagination that her smile appeared both slightly sad, and strained. "Now rest. One of us will be nearby if you should need anything."

With that she picked up the tray and walked toward the door. She opened it and paused only a moment, turning to regard the viscount before she exited the room. She surprised both of them by saying, as she did so, "Pleasant dreams."

Chapter
Six

Viscount Chalmsy could not really call his dreams pleasant, interrupted as they were from time to time by visions of the lovely Cressida Carrington, who each time she seemed to be approaching him, was sent off another way by her older sister, who always turned and shook her head at Jack in the most remonstrative manner, Miss Carrington's upper lip rising slightly in a way Jack had never seen her do.

The viscount's dream self was further confused when he realized that that slightly raised upper lip was actually a trick of his own, used to convey mockery and contempt. It had always worked perfectly well for Viscount Chalmsy, but he was disturbed in his dreams to find Miss Carrington regarding him with contempt—not that he cared what the woman thought of him, his dream self assured him, but still—still—

The question of why Miss Carrington would not want him to fall in love with her sister in the hopes it would lead to matrimony so puzzled Jack that when he next encountered Cressida Carrington in his dreams, he blurted out, "Why wouldn't your sister want you to marry me?"

Unfortunately, it was only after he had said the words that Jack realized he was no longer asleep, a realization that made him fall back upon his pillows with a groan, wondering what had happened to his usual sangfroid.

Happily for the viscount, Cressida did not seem to find the question as untoward as he thought it, nor did she seem at all aware that the color in his face was much redder than his normal complexion. Instead of regarding him as if he had lost his mind, or blushing and stammering some nonsensical answer, she fixed him with her angelic blue eyes and said, without the slightest hesitation, "Because we would not suit, my lord. Surely you see that?"

Jack did see it, but was not so ready to admit the Misses Carrington might see it, too. Didn't they know most women were on the lookout for the most advantageous match possible, and the devil take suitability?

"I am considered quite a good catch, you know," he said.

Cressida smiled and said she was sure he was.

"Then why—"

Cressida's smile grew. "But money and appearance and position are not everything, are they, my lord?"

Viscount Chalmsy, much accustomed to people to whom money and appearance and position *were* everything, quirked an eyebrow. Cressida said gently, as if explaining to a child, that happiness was worth much, much more. And Julia would always want her brothers and sisters to be happy.

"Well, yes," Jack said, thinking aloud, "but what happiness has to do with marriage—"

He was suddenly aware that the young lady was regarding him with surprise, and said hastily, "That is—"

With a testiness he had not before believed he possessed, the viscount returned to his original question. "Why wouldn't your sister wish you to marry me? I'll have you know there are any number of women who think I'd make them blissfully happy. Certainly their mamas think my offering for one of their beautiful daughters would make *them* very happy! I've been meeting and avoiding them—hopeful daughters and even more hopeful mamas!—for years, drat it! So what's wrong with me?"

Julia Carrington would have told him—would have made him a list, he was sure—but Cressida possessed neither her sister's sharp tongue nor her strength of character. Instead the lovely young woman said in her soft voice that it was not that there was anything wrong with the viscount; it was just that they would not suit.

"For I am of a very biddable nature, you know," Cressida told him wisely, "and Julia says men such as you should never marry biddable wives. You need a woman who will stand up to you." She regarded him critically, saw the thunder in his brow, and added, her face thoughtful, "I daresay she is right."

"Oh, you do, do you?" Jack glared at her, then tempered his glare as he saw her draw back in surprise. It occurred to Jack that most men probably did not glare at the lovely Cressida.

"Well," he told her, with a tight smile that did not reach his eyes, "you may tell your sister for me that I *should too* marry a biddable wife. Every man should. A very, very biddable wife—not that I wish for a wife, because I don't, but if I did, I should want her to be very biddable, and not some strong-minded female forever baiting and haranguing me—"

He was stopped by Cressida's sudden giggle, and his face grew suspicious as he asked what was wrong. The girl informed him with great kindness that Julia had said his lordship was cross as a bear, and Cressida could see her sister was right.

"It is because of your injuries, you see," she explained, when the viscount appeared to in no way appreciate her comment. "And your cold."

"Oh, it is, is it?" the viscount fumed, rubbing his watery eyes and aware all at once of the picture he must present, with his reddened nose and frequent cough. "Is that what your sister says? Well, let me tell you, Miss Carrington, and you may tell your sister that a saint—a *saint!*—would be cross as a bear if he found himself in my situation, being prosed and preached at, and having nasty-tasting medicine tipped down my throat when I open my mouth, and—and—"

Cressida made several soothing comments before adding, after considerable cogitation, that if he did not mind very much, she would rather not relay that message to her sister, for Julia might think it was meant as a criticism, and Cressida knew the viscount could not be meaning to criticize dear Julia . . . .

The martial light in the viscount's eye suggested that might very well be his purpose and Cressida, not wishing to upset him further, suddenly remembered the errand that had brought her to his room. Her smile was conciliatory as she said, "Oh, dear! Silly me! I have quite forgotten to tell you about your visitor!"

"Visitor?" Jack, who in his mind had been forming other scathing messages Cressida might carry to Julia Carrington, frowned. "Visitor? Oh." He thought he knew, and his mouth turned down. "If it's that Smythley character, I'm not going to have him prodding and poking me again today, and he might as well leave now, which you can tell him!"

"No, no!" Cressida soothed, smiling to think how much he would appreciate her news. "It is not Dr. Smythley at all! Your brother has come!"

"Charles?" Jack sat up with an eagerness that Cressida found most appropriate for one hearing of his brother's arrival. Unfortunately, the viscount's much-jostled muscles did not approve of his enthusiasm nearly as much as Cressida Carrington did, and he sank back onto the pillows again with a groan.

"Poor Viscount Chalmsy," Cressida sympathized.

The viscount ignored her. "Where is he?" he demanded. "Bring him up at once!"

Cressida said she would, now that she had ascertained that the viscount was awake, as Julia had bade her do while the viscount's brother took a cup of tea and a piece of shepherd's pie, something Miss Carrington was bound he must do after hearing he had left town immediately upon hearing of his brother's injury, without even stopping for a bite, or to pack a bag.

"He did that, did he?" Jack asked, trying to cover the rough emotion in his voice with a cough.

Cressida nodded. "Julia," she informed him, "says you have a wonderful brother. She says he feels just as he ought. She says you are very lucky to have him. She says—"

Cressida stopped suddenly and Jack saw pink tinge her cheeks as she said she would just go fetch Mr. Charles Carlesworth, then.

Jack glared. "She says I don't deserve him, doesn't she?" he demanded. He knew he'd guessed right when the girl's pink cheeks turned red.

"I should not have . . . " Cressida stammered.

"Think nothing of it, Miss Carrington," Jack said, his eyes and the taut muscles of his face at odds with his tone. "It is not you who shouldn't have—it's your sister!"

Cressida, not knowing what to say, said nothing, and fled.

"Ah," said Jack affably when the door to his room next opened and Julia Carrington ushered Charles through it. "The brother I don't deserve!"

Mr. Carlesworth, surprised by the words but thinking them just Jack's odd way, said, by way of greeting, "You're alive then, Jack!" and moved forward.

The viscount, however glad he might be to see his brother, was not at the moment looking at him; he was watching Miss Carrington to see what effect his statement had on her. He was considerably gratified when he saw her check for a moment, and shoot him a swift glance from eyes that immediately were lowered.

When the lady looked up again she was smiling brightly and said, with a smoothness Jack had to grudgingly admire, "I am glad to see you recognize your good fortune, my lord! Perhaps it takes a fever to make a man see such things, and appreciate the gifts given him! It does credit to your good sense, something I was not aware you had a store of!"

Charles, surprised by the tightening of his brother's jaw, looked around toward Miss Carrington in puzzlement. Her smile was kind as she said, "Well, I shall just leave the two of you together, then!" and whisked herself out of the room. Charles returned his gaze to his brother's.

"An excellent woman, Miss Carrington," Mr. Carlesworth said, only to be taken aback by the viscount's rather savage echoing of the word "excellent."

Charles eyed his brother consideringly. "Ah," Mr. Carlesworth said, nodding. "Put you in one of your pets, has she?"

The savageness in his voice did not abate as Jack said he did not take pets. Ever.

The viscount's brother incensed him by laughing. "When it was one of your pets that put you on the road the day you were injured—" Charles said.

Jack, who only that morning had said the same thing to Edward, rebutted the statement immediately, saying it was no such thing. Charles looked at him, then grinned.

"I'm awfully glad you didn't stick your spoon in the wall, old boy," Charles said, putting a hand affectionately, if briefly, around his brother's neck, and considerably discomposing the viscount by doing so.

"Yes, well—" Jack said. He raised his shoulders in a slight shrug. "As for that, I expect I've robbed you of a chance to be viscount."

They grinned at each other and, their transports complete, sat for several moments in comfortable silence, Charles perched on the side of the bed as Jack lay back against his pillows.

"Grandfather wanted to come, but his back is acting up a bit, with the weather," Charles said, anxious that his brother not believe he had been slighted by the family. "Arabella and I persuaded him it would be better for me to come, since the message we received said your accident was not believed to be of a terribly serious nature."

"Oh, is that what the message said?" Jack asked, aware that if his injuries had been portrayed as more serious he would have been incensed, yet irrationally angered to learn that they had not been. He coughed, and swore under his breath at the jolting that action gave his ribs.

Charles looked at him anxiously. "You aren't terribly hurt, are you?"

Jack shook his head. "No, no," he said. "Just a bump on the head and an ankle that will have me laid up for a while, and every muscle in my body feeling as if it had been pummeled in the ring! Plus this miserable head cold has me cross as a bear."

Charles nodded. "That is what Miss Carrington said."

The satisfaction of Mr. Carlesworth's face was not echoed on Jack's as Charles, unheeding, continued. "Arabella was quite upset she could not come, but young Jack just yesterday started throwing out spots, and the doctor says it is chicken pox, and of course the boy wants his mama, so—"

"Well, thank goodness for that!" Jack interrupted, saw the startled look of reproach on his brother's face, and said at once that it wasn't that he was glad his nephew had the chicken pox, far from it, but at least young Jack's misfortune had kept the poor boy's fond mama from descending on the hapless viscount.

Charles grinned, but shook his head in remonstrance, saying that Jack did not appropriately appreciate the solicitations of his devoted family. The viscount agreed. Devoutly. Then he asked his solicitous brother to at once remove him from the Carrington household.

He was stunned by Mr. Carlesworth's reply.

"But Jack," Charles said, blinking at him in surprise. "I can't!"

"What?" Jack bounded up off his pillows, then found himself collapsing back upon them in frustration and immediate pain. "What do you mean you cannot?"

Charles surprise grew. "Miss Carrington says the doctor has said you must not leave this room for at least a week!" Charles told him, ever reasonable. "And the man would not really recommend traveling for another week or two after that, depending on how your ankle does! And of course we can't chance having that cold go to your lungs and develop into pneumonia! Surely you see that."

The viscount, with whom such pieces of information had not before been shared, uttered an expletive his brother had not heard for years.

"Jack!" Charles remonstrated, shocked.

"That's nonsense!" the viscount said. "Pure and utter nonsense! I could go today—I *will* go today! The doctor is a quack, and Miss Carrington much too busy about my business! So I've got a few bruises, and my head feels like it's stuffed with wet cotton! I'm not about to come down with pneumonia if you move me—it would please Miss Carrington and your despicable wife far too much to be able to say 'I told you so,' and I won't give them the satisfaction. So just pile me into the carriage—"

It was there that the viscount suffered another check. Charles, shaking his head at his brother, could only inform Viscount Chalmsy that he had left town on horseback, that being the quickest way he knew to travel, and had not brought the carriage, so he could not possibly carry Jack away.

"But you could return to town and get it!" Jack said. "Be back tomorrow!"

Charles said consideringly that he *could* do so, but he hardly felt that would be the best thing. His brother goggled at him. Then he pleaded. Then he cajoled. Then he threatened. All to no avail.

Jack had resorted to sulky silence by the time Charles said he must return to town that very night, with young Jack also sick and Arabella so worried, but on the way back Mr. Carlesworth would call on Dr. Smythley and see what the man had to say. If the doctor thought it would be all right for Jack to travel . . .

Charles let the sentence trail off as Jack twitched one of the pillows out from behind his head and wadded it up, then heaved it at his brother. The viscount groaned at the pain that movement caused, but felt it was worth it.

Viscount Chalmsy had no doubt what the doctor would say. He was pretty certain that the doctor *liked* treating a viscount, leaders of the ton not often coming Dr. Smythley's way, and Jack was convinced the man of medicine would keep the viscount as a patient as long as possible. Jack also knew that if his brother was told the viscount should not travel, Charles would make no move to help Jack do something Charles—and, the viscount thought suddenly, Miss Carrington—would say was too foolish for words.

Mr. Carlesworth dodged the pillow, then returned it to his brother. His gaze was sympathetic as he asked Jack if there were any messages the viscount wished carried back to London, or anything Charles could send his brother from town. Jack opened one eye, then closed it again, turning his back on his brother.

"Tell Grandfather not to worry," Jack said, as he heard Charles's steady tread moving toward the door. "Tell Arabella it's all her fault. Tell yourself what a scaly fellow you are, for leaving your only brother like this. And send me John. And Phipps."

Chapter
Seven

The viscount awakened the next morning to the pleasant aroma of coffee, brewed just as he liked it. He turned appreciatively toward the smell and opened his eyes to find his valet standing beside his bed, a steaming cup in hand.

"Phipps!" Jack said, sure he had never been so glad to see anyone in his life. All his valet's shortcomings and pomposities were forgotten as the viscount stared up at the man in wholehearted delight. "You've come, then!"

Phipps presented the coffee with a slight bow and the pleasing information that he was glad to see his lordship as well as he did. Jack, sipping the brew as if it were elixir, said his valet wasn't half as happy to see Jack as Jack was to see him.

"Civilization," the viscount said, looking approvingly upon his servant. "That's what you are, Phipps. An oasis of civilization in the desert of my misery. Is John with you?"

Pleased with his analogy, the viscount nodded when told his groom was seeing to the horses before calling upon his lordship. Viscount Chalmsy sipped his coffee for several moments in pleasurable silence before he noticed the rather somber expression his remark about Phipps's presence had occasioned on the valet's face.

"Well, man?" Jack said, expecting to hear Phipps had already discovered the condition of Jack's badly mangled boots—a condition that had made Jack himself blanch, when Miss Carrington had brought them out for his inspection the night before at his demand. Jack expected to hear that it was not what the valet was used to; he expected to hear that the man feared he would never be the same again. What he did not expect to hear was that Phipps was leaving him.

"*What*?" Jack said, splashing hot coffee on himself when he jerked upright after the valet's announcement, and cursing roundly because of it.

Mr. Phipps thoughtfully removed the coffee from his lordship's suddenly slackened hold before repeating his words. "I regret to inform you, sir, that I am leaving your service. I have just come down to do so, me not thinking it right to just send word with John—"

"Well, I should say it dashedly *wouldn't* be right!" Jack told him, irritation apparent in his voice and in the way he ran his hand through his hair, then sneezed. "And it isn't right to come to tell me, either! It isn't right to leave me at all! Especially now, when I'm injured and ailing. *That's* what isn't *right*, Phipps! For goodness' sake, man, I'm sorry about the boots, but it wasn't something I had control over, and one has to learn to let such things go. There will be other boots, you know. Even better ones!"

Mr. Phipps disclaimed any knowledge of boots, and took a step back as if he feared the viscount might be raging out of his mind with fever. Jack glared at him for several minutes before uttering a very petulant, "Well, what is it, then?"

The prim-faced valet explained that after the viscount had left town—that very afternoon, in fact—Phipps was out

making those few purchases necessary to replenish his lordship's wardrobe when he had encountered Lord Marblethorpe at that shop only the most discriminating choose
for their cravats. Lord Marblethorpe had been much astounded to hear, upon inquiring as to Viscount Chalmsy's
health, that the viscount had just that day gone out of
town—without his valet. Lord Marblethorpe had made it
clear that he himself would never set foot outside the city
without his man—if he had a man, having just had to let his
current fellow go, because of the condition of Lord Marblethorpe's cravats, and a thumbprint found on one of his
lordship's boots.

"*Cravats?*" Jack repeated, still stunned by the news of
Phipps's perfidity. "*Boots?*"

The valet nodded. "His lordship said the man just didn't
have a way with them; his lordship's cravats were never
quite as they should be, and as for his boots—well! The man
just couldn't get them to shine as his lordship felt they
should. And then when his lordship found a smudged fin-
gerprint on a boot—oh, I was never so shocked in my life as
to hear that, for any valet worth his salt, I told his lordship,
and begged his pardon for speaking so plainly with him, but
any valet who would so far forget himself as to not wear
gloves and remove any telltale signs that the boots had in
any way been touched by human hands—well, I told his
lordship, that man is not worthy of the brotherhood of
valets! Lord Marblethorpe agreed, as if much struck by what
I'd said, and then he just happened to mention how *your*
boots are the envy of all of London, and he said quite kindly
that he knew that was because of my work, and—well—one
thing led to another . . . ."

"Are you telling me Lord Marblethorpe is stealing you

from me because of the shine on my *boots*?" Viscount Chalmsy asked, much incensed.

A fair-minded Phipps said that he wouldn't categorize it as *stealing*, really; but his lordship *had* made a very flattering offer, and what with Lord Marblethorpe feeling just as he ought about the importance of never traveling without his valet—

"Phipps," Jack said, in a voice that made the valet rather glad the viscount could not at that moment rise from his bed, "I believe you forget yourself! Marblethorpe is a nodcock— everyone knows it! Of *course* he wouldn't leave the city without his man—and several other servants, I'm sure! He needs them to find the way back for him! *I*, on the other hand, am not such a namby-pamby as to need a valet to care for me every time I choose to jaunt out of the city."

Phipps looked down his long nose at the viscount. "That is as it may be, sir," he said, each word precise as it tripped smoothly from between his thin lips, "but there—you were hale and hearty before you left London, weren't you?"

On that unarguable note the valet took his leave, wishing the speechless viscount a speedy recovery and saying he trusted all soon would be well with his lordship. As he opened the bedroom door he promised to send John up to help the viscount ready himself for the day.

"John?" the viscount repeated. *"John?"*

Miss Carrington, entering as Phipps made his exit, heard the last of their exchange. She smiled wickedly at Viscount Chalmsy and said, in a tone of hearty encouragement, "I am sure your John will be excellent with you, my lord." Her eyes twinkled. "After all, Edward has just told me the man has a way with even the most recalcitrant of horses!"

She managed to just dodge the pillow Jack heaved at her,

relenting enough to return it to him before she quit the room. As she tucked it behind his head she said, "Poor Viscount, you have already had quite a morning, haven't you—and it's not yet nine o'clock!" in such a commiserating tone that Jack could not be totally angry with her, try as he might.

"So you know, do you?" The viscount humphed, frowning up at her as she plumped his pillows to her satisfaction and paused to feel his forehead for a moment. With a thoughtfulness he could not help but appreciate she handed him a fresh handkerchief, then looked politely away as he blew his nose.

"Of course." Miss Carrington's reply to his question was tranquil. "It is my duty to know what occurs in my home— with two younger brothers and two younger sisters, it is not only my duty, it is my salvation! What would be even better would be not only to know what occurs, but what *might* occur. I have not perfected that yet. . . . "

She stood above him for a moment, her head tilted slightly to the side as if she considered her last words and puzzled over why she could not totally predict the future.

"Can you *sometimes* tell what will occur?" Jack asked, partly because he was intrigued, and partly because he did not wish her to leave. *That*, he told himself, was because he was in need of human company after his valet's unceremonious and unfeeling departure from Jack's sinking ship. And it seemed Miss Carrington had a way of making him feel better—more peaceful, perhaps—when she was nearby. Not that Jack chose to follow that thought down any particular path where it might lead. . . .

Miss Carrington looked down at him in surprise, glancing from her hand, which he had captured with one of his, to his face. Her lips turned up, and her eyes twinkled.

"Oh, yes, my lord," she told him, "I certainly can! For instance, when the vicar arrives I can predict almost without fail that if the man stays more than half an hour and has conversation with William during that time, William will be moved to do something quite outrageous, if I cannot forestall him. And I can predict that if Lily happens upon the cherry tarts while cook is out of the kitchen there will be none left for dinner, and I will have a very sick child on my hands! I know that if any impressionable young man wanders into Cressida's orbit his intellect—if he had any to begin with—probably will be knocked to flinders, and I know that having a viscount in the house will inspire Edward to cut a dash that likely will lead to all sorts of foolish behavior—"

Jack's promise to try to keep Edward from foolish behavior made the lady look down at him strangely. "Yes, well," she said, almost as it to herself, "I'm sure it is very good of you to offer, my lord, but really, given the circumstances . . ."

Her words trailed off and Jack realized belatedly that she did not think the behavior that had brought the viscount to her home was what she wanted her brother to emulate. He said with a sniff that he supposed he knew how to take *that*, then.

"Oh, I'm sure you do," the lady replied, smiling seraphically as Jack's brow darkened.

"Well, of all the rude—" Jack began, only to be interrupted when Miss Carrington quite cordially agreed with him.

"Yes," she said. "But totally irresistible, believe me! I could not refrain, knowing what your reaction would be!"

Jack, astounded by her words, gave her one incredulous

glance before narrowing his eyes and staring up at her with a hard look that had been known to make more than one man remove himself from the viscount's path. Miss Carrington remained singularly unmoved.

"Are you telling me you were baiting me again?" he asked. "That you know how I will react, and you—you—"

Words failed him as Miss Carrington laughed. "I must apologize, I see," she said, then shook her head reproachfully at him. "Although part of the blame is yours, you know; as I told you once before, you are simply too *easy* to bait!"

Jack, who had spent his life building a reputation as a man other men did not care to bother, could only stare at her. When she was sure he had no more to say Miss Carrington promised, in the kindest manner possible, to send the viscount's groom, John, up to him as soon as the man was done with the horses, his more important patients.

This time the pillow the viscount aimed at her caught her between the shoulder blades as she neared the door. The lady did not look back but Jack was sure that, as she closed the door, he heard her giggle.

The viscount awoke that afternoon in a foul temper. His interview with his groom had not gone as he'd expected, for while John said that he had every intention of remaining at Carrington Place until the viscount could travel, the groom showed no inclination to believe Jack's assertion that he could travel that very day.

In fact John, who had been with Jack since he set up in town, and who had worked for Jack's grandfather during Jack's growing up at High Point, said bluntly that Jack's brother and grandfather had instructed the groom in no uncertain terms that he was not to let the viscount do anything foolish, and that he was to see that Jack stayed put and healed properly and did not leave until the doctor and that nice Miss Carrington agreed that the viscount was well enough to travel.

"That *nice Miss Carrington*?" Jack repeated, feeling as if a vein in his head might pop. He stared at his henchman in astonishment. "That *nice Miss Carrington* is a meddling, stubborn, sharp-tongued wretch! A virago! A—a—"

"Now, my lord," John said, in the voice he'd used when Jack was a recalcitrant ten-year-old. "Miss Carrington is a real lady, and your brother was much taken with her common sense. He said that she is a woman who feels just as she ought, and that he was only sorry you should be such a burden on her."

"Such a—such a—"

Jack gave up trying to complete that sentence, and contented himself with a vehemently delivered tirade on how his brother was certainly no judge of women, having never been much in their way, and having chosen a virago for his own wife. The fact that what he said was punctuated with sneezes and sniffles in no way discomposed John, but the viscount's last words the groom could not allow. John said with a reproachful shake of his head that his lordship was clearly out of sorts, for Mr. Carlesworth's wife was everything a lady should be.

"*Arabella?*" Jack shouted.

John nodded, and said with a wisdom that his master in no way appreciated that the problem was that Viscount Chalmsy was not used to running to rein, him being so headstrong and all. For that reason John thought it rare good fortune that that nice Miss Carrington seemed to be able to

handle several sets of reins at once—for it was clear it was
she who had the raising of her brothers and sisters, after
all—and to bring them all off safely.

Jack let it be known that he had no intention of running to
anyone's rein but his own, and added that if John, or Jack's
brother, or his sister-in-law, or even his grandfather, and *certainly* if that *managing* Miss Carrington thought to change
that, they had better think again. And quickly.

John's tolerant assertion that his lordship always had been
that way only ignited the viscount's temper further. When
his groom turned a deaf ear to the viscount's arguments as
to why they should remove from Carrington Place immediately, saying only that the grays needed his attention, Jack
gnashed his teeth. Then John added, to Jack's considerable
vexation, that the horses were dealing much more intelligently with the results of the accident than their owner was
because the horses knew when to stay quiet and be taken
care of.

"But I don't want to be taken care of, confound it!" Jack
shouted, earning him a "Too resty by half" comment and a
reproachful headshake from his groom.

In anger Jack had said that his groom worked for *him*, and
not for his brother or grandfather, and if the man liked his
job . . .

He had let the threat hang between them, but since they
both knew it was an empty one, John's reply was no more
than another headshake, and the advice that his lordship get
some sleep and see if he could wake up feeling more the
thing. The viscount, frustrated on all sides in his plans to return to London as quickly as possible, grunted and turned
pointedly away from the groom. He was considerably frustrated when John, far from feeling bad at his master's dis-

pleasure, only chuckled and left the room a few moments later, whistling.

The viscount awoke with a dull ache in both his head and ankle, and several other muscles protested as he turned to try to find a more comfortable position. His dreams had not been pleasant ones, for in his sleep he had relived the accident, seeing the children in the road, trying to turn the horses, feeling himself fall—

He had awakened with a start, and now realized he was sweating. As he put an impatient hand to his forehead a movement near the window caught his eye, and he turned fully so he could see the figure standing there. It was the little girl named Lily, who had a propensity for bursting into tears at sight of him. Jack groaned, then was sorry he had as a look of trepidation crossed her face.

"No," Jack said, waving a weary hand in her direction. "I am not going to die."

The little girl smiled and walked softly forward, until she stood at the side of his bed. Her serious young eyes focused on his face.

"Are you sure?" she asked him. She stood with her hands behind her back, and Jack eyed her in exasperation.

"My dear girl," he said, "what is this fascination you have with my impending doom?"

He was immediately sorry for his sarcastic tone, for tears welled up in the child's eyes and slid unheeded down her cheeks.

"Oh, for goodness' sake!" Jack said, reaching out with the corner of his bedsheet to wipe her face. "I'm sorry, child! I did not mean to make you cry! Stop now, and I'll—I'll—"

He had no idea what might stop a six-year-old girl from crying, so in desperation he tried, "I'll tell you a story."

Lily blinked several times, and allowed him to wipe her face again.

"What kind of story?" she asked, surprising him by sitting down on the bed. Her hands came out from behind her back and she held one toward him with a simple, "Here."

Jack looked down at a badly mangled cherry tart, then up into her face.

"I brought it for you," Lily said.

"Well!" Jack looked at the cherry juice smeared on her hands and gingerly took the offering, sniffing it for a moment before he valiantly popped it into his mouth and tried not to think of how it had come by its bedraggled appearance. He was rewarded by a sudden smile, and the confidence that cherry tarts were Lily's favorite.

Jack smacked his lips and said he rather believed they were *his* favorite, too. That earned him another smile.

She was an appealing child, Jack thought suddenly—when she wasn't crying all over him. She had her sister Cressida's coloring, but there was something in the way she held her head, and that questioning look in her eyes that spoke of the elder Miss Carrington. Not that Jack could imagine Miss Carrington as a watering pot, even at age six. She, he was sure, had come into the world in command and unshakable, staring at all around her with a calm demeanor from the moment she left the womb. Although every now and then, the viscount did think he glimpsed in Miss Carrington's dark brown eyes a hint of a younger, more carefree and quite flusterable Julia. . . .

Right now a younger version of Miss Carrington's eyes were regarding him expectantly, and Jack could not remember why. Lily seemed to realize that, for she prompted him with a shy "What kind of story are you going to tell me, my lord?"

Passing under quick review all the stories that had come his way in the past year, Jack could find none that he believed appropriate for a child. He stalled with, "Well, what kind of stories do you like?"

Lily told him she liked all kinds, and then, watching his face carefully and apparently feeling she had not been particularly helpful, added, "I like stories about animals."

Jack nodded.

"Animals," he said, rubbing his chin and watching her. She nodded in return. When he sneezed she handed him her handkerchief in the most matter-of-fact way possible, and the action made him smile as he accepted her offering with grave thanks. That was a replica of the eldest Miss Carrington, through and through—seeing a need and filling it as a matter of course.

"Animals, you say? Hmmm . . . "

Jack rubbed his chin again and, after clearing his throat several times, began. "Once there was a horse—oh, a noble, shining horse—who loved to run. He could run faster than all the other horses in England, although the other horses didn't know it, and were always trying to catch him. One day the horse heard of a place where horses went to run, a magical kingdom called Newmarket—"

His story was interrupted by the entrance of Julia Carrington, who walked quietly into the room and stopped just by the door at the sight that greeted her.

"Lily?" the lady said, coming forward, her head tilted slightly to the side, a questioning note in her voice. Jack smiled to notice her youngest sister's head immediately tilted to the same angle. "What are you doing here, my dear?"

Lily said that she was keeping his lordship company, so that he would not be lonely. That, Miss Carrington noted, seemed a surprise to the viscount, but he recovered quickly, meeting Julia's look with a bland one of his own.

"Oh, and Julia," the little girl continued, her blond curls dancing, her eyes alight with excitement, "he is telling me the most wonderful story, about a shining horse who loves to run, and who is going to a magical kingdom named Newmarket—"

"Newmarket?" Miss Carrington appeared to suffer from a sudden tickle in her throat, for she coughed several times, then said, "My lord! Really!" in a tone that made Lily look at her inquiringly. The viscount had the grace to redden, and directed his attention toward the window.

Miss Carrington lifted her sister down from the bed and told her to run along now, and let his lordship sleep. She added kindly that she believed cook was making cherry tarts, and Lily might tell her Julia had said the little girl could have one. Something in the expression on Lily's face made Miss Carrington amend her statement, "But you already knew that, didn't you, Lily?"

The child glanced up and gave her a swift smile, then started toward the door.

"How many did you take, Lily?" Miss Carrington called after her. The child turned and said conscientiously that she had given his lordship, the viscount, one.

"Oh?" Miss Carrington turned toward Lord Chalmsy for verification, and smiled at his nod. "Well, that is very nice, but how many others—" she said as she turned back toward her little sister, then stopped when she realized she was addressing a quietly closing door. She smiled.

"I suppose," she said thoughtfully, "that we really ought to make apple tarts, instead."

"Oh, no!" the viscount protested from his bed. "Cherry tarts are our favorite!"

He was rewarded with a laugh, and grinned as Miss Carrington turned back toward him.

"I hope, my lord," she said, coming forward and standing at the foot of his bed, "that Lily has not tired you too much, or been a nuisance. I have told the children you need your rest, but Lily—" She shrugged.

Even more to his surprise than to hers, the viscount said that the child had been no bother; in fact, she was rather taking, and he thought her visit made him feel better. That modicum of praise won him a beaming smile from Miss Carrington, who said he was kind to say so, but in the future she would instruct Lily not to visit him.

"But no!" Lord Chalmsy protested, surprising himself even more. "She is good company. Although it *is* a start to wake up and find her staring at me, close at hand. And I wouldn't wish her to catch this infernal cold, after all."

Julia said she would take care of the close-up staring, and she really didn't think the children would take the viscount's cold from him now. She started back toward the door, saying over her shoulder that she had only come to see if he needed anything, and if he did not, she had many other things to do. . . .

The viscount stopped her with an abrupt, "Why is the child so afraid I will die, Miss Carrington?"

For a moment he did not think the lady would respond. She stood, still facing the door, and he saw her shoulders slump before she turned to take several steps back toward him, her eyes sad. When she again reached the foot of the bed she looked at him and said, "That is still troubling her, isn't it?"

At the viscount's nod she sighed and rubbed her brow, as if trying to erase a hurt that lingered there. "Poor Lily," she said softly. The viscount waited.

"You see, my lord," Miss Carrington said, moving from the foot of the bed to the chair beside it, and sinking down there, "four years ago our father . . . " Jack saw the sadness in her eyes grow more pronounced. "Our father was killed in a carriage accident."

"I'm sorry," Jack said. Miss Carrington nodded.

"Lily," she said, "well, I don't know how much of Father Lily even remembers, but when you were injured—"

Jack nodded. "I see," he said.

"Lily has a great fear of carriages," Miss Carrington said, rubbing her forehead again. Jack was sure she was unaware of the action. "She does not understand." She sighed again and sat for several moments before rising to say, with something approaching her normal briskness, that if there was nothing else—

"And your mother?" Jack asked suddenly.

Miss Carrington looked at him in surprise.

"Mother," she said after a moment, in a carefully neutral tone that revealed much more than it concealed from someone as adept at hiding his feelings as the viscount was, "is with her sister, Delia, at the moment. She is often there. My aunt Delia—" She started as if she would say one thing, then amended it to "—is not well."

Jack, watching her closely, said, "Isn't, or thinks she isn't?"

Miss Carrington looked startled, then a rueful smile touched her lips. "Oh, dear," she said. "Was I that obvious?"

The viscount grinned. "I have known any number of Aunt Delias, I'm afraid."

Miss Carrington sighed. "I should not be so harsh," she said. "Mother certainly thinks she is ill. Mother thinks they are *all* ill. . . . "

At his inquiring gaze Julia explained that her mother had seven sisters, and was often called to tend one or the other of them.

"But what about her own family?" the viscount asked. Miss Carrington smiled.

"Oh, you need not worry for us, my lord," she assured him. "Sometimes I think we remind Mother so much of Father, and she still misses him so. Perhaps she is more happy to go away from us than one might think—" Julia stopped, as if surprised by the words slipping from her lips.

"That is—" Miss Carrington smiled down at him. "We all have each other, after all, and the children have me. We all miss Mother when she is gone, of course, but I explain to the little ones. . . . "

Her words trailed off, and the look on her face suggested there were things even the redoubtable Miss Carrington could not explain.

"So you are in charge of everything." The viscount said the words abruptly, and Miss Carrington looked at him in surprise. Then she smiled.

"Not everything, my lord," she said. "I leave a *bit* of business to the king and Parliament!"

The viscount would not be distracted. "It is a great deal of responsibility for someone so young," he said, his frown deepening.

Miss Carrington interpreted the frown as a sign of criticism, and said stiffly that it need not concern him; and besides, she was not so young as he might think her. Viscount Chalmsy, reacting to the stiffness in her voice, grinned.

"A veritable dowager," he suggested. Miss Carrington glared.

"Is there no one else to help you?" he asked. Julia nodded.

"Well, yes," she said. "Of course. We are not totally alone in the world. Our servants are quite loyal to us. And we have Uncle William."

"Uncle William?" It seemed odd—very odd—to the viscount that any uncle in the house or anywhere in the vicinity had not called upon him, since Lord Chalmsy was a guest under the Carrington roof, and Edward had made it clear that the viscount's reputation had preceded him into the neighborhood. After a moment Jack said in as neutral a voice as he could muster that he would like to meet her uncle—at the man's convenience, of course.

Miss Carrington shook her head. "I am sorry to disappoint you, my lord," she said, and once again that tranquil expression was set in her eyes. "But I am afraid it is not at all convenient. Uncle William is not with us just now. Uncle William is at sea."

Chapter
Eight

"At *sea?*" Jack repeated. His startled response provoked a coughing spell, and it was several moments before he could continue. When he did, he was glaring at Miss Carrington. Again. "At *sea*?? Well, what good is an uncle *at sea*? It's not as if he's here to help you."

Miss Carrington said in the tranquil manner Viscount Chalmsy was coming to recognize as so much her own that they could hardly expect Uncle William to change his life simply because his brother had had the bad manners to get himself killed in a carriage accident.

"Bad manners—" Jack repeated, staring at her in the most peculiar way, his mouth hanging slightly agape. He snapped it shut, then asked again just what her uncle thought he was doing, being at sea?

Miss Carrington said with great reasonableness that her uncle was a sea captain; where else would he be?

Jack's frown grew. "Well, he might be here with you," he said with some asperity. "Stop being noble, girl, and think! There are other ways to make a living than going to sea!"

"Yes," Miss Carrington said, with the same reasonableness, "but not for a sea captain."

Jack ran a distracted hand through his hair. "Surely there are other things he could do."

Miss Carrington shook her head. "It has always been the sea for Uncle William," she said. "Always. But you mustn't think he ignores us. When he is in port and has the time between voyages, he comes to visit us. And two years ago he took Edward up to London for a fortnight, showing him the sights. That's where Edward saw you, you know," she said, nodding at him as if it were the most commonplace thing they were discussing, and not the actions of an uncle and mother who had left extremely heavy duties on her shoulders.

"How often does this uncle visit?" Jack asked. "And how long has your mother been with her sister?" His voice raised as his frown deepened, and Miss Carrington stared thoughtfully at him.

"Really, my lord," she said, "you are upsetting yourself over nothing. We do well enough, and Mother and Uncle William do the best they can."

"I am not upset!" Jack snapped, ignoring her knowing smile but lowering his voice when he heard how loud he'd become. He reached for his handkerchief, and blew his nose with a vengeance. "How often, and how long?"

"I beg your pardon?"

Jack, fairly sure the lady was skirting his question on purpose, clung to it like a bulldog. "How often does your uncle visit?" he asked. "When was he last here?"

Miss Carrington plumped his pillows once, and repeated that it was none of the viscount's concern. In a gentle voice she suggested that he try to get some sleep.

"When?" Jack asked, catching her wrist and holding on to it. She looked down at his strong tapered fingers for a moment, then gently pried them away with her other hand.

When Jack made no further attempt to delay her she

walked to the door, pausing there only to say, "I hope you have a pleasant rest, my lord. And you must not concern yourself with us. As I said before, we do well enough."

"When?" Jack repeated, the word almost a croak as he coughed it.

The lady sighed, and opened the door. "Two years ago," she said, not looking at him as she slipped through it. "Two years. But Mother has only been gone six weeks, so I imagine we will see her within a month or two. Certainly, without fail, by Christmas."

Angry on the lady's behalf, Jack took up their uncle's protracted absence with Edward when that young gentleman poked his head into the viscount's room just before supper to ask if there was anything he might do for Lord Chalmsy. Since John was with the viscount at the moment it might have seemed a futile offer, but Jack, seeing an opportunity to learn more about the Carrington household, sent John off to check on the grays—something his servant had just done before coming to attend the viscount, which John pointed out as if his lordship had lost his mind. After the groom took his grumbling leave Jack told Edward that he could give him a cup of water, if he would be so kind.

Edward was eager to do so and eager to answer any questions the viscount might put to him. Truth be told, Edward was eager just to spend time with the viscount. He slipped into the chair by Jack's bed when Jack invited him to do so, and gave every appearance of being ready to visit forever, if the viscount should so desire.

It was clear to Lord Chalmsy that the young man did not think there was anything so very odd in his uncle's behavior. Edward told the viscount, when pressed, that Julia had

explained to them all that they could not ask Uncle
William to leave the sea just because they might like him
to do so, and that while he was named with their mother as
the children's guardian, they weren't to be a burden on
him, when it certainly wasn't Uncle William's fault their
father had met with his accident. Uncle William had been
quite torn up about their father's death, when next he visited them.

That, Jack learned, had been nearly ten months after the
Carrington's father died, Uncle William having been at sea
all over the globe, and the careful letter Julia wrote him
never having caught up with him.

"I take it you like your uncle William," Jack said, watching the young man's face. Edward said cheerfully that his
uncle was a great gun; in fact, Edward rather thought the
viscount was quite like him.

"Oh?" Jack sat up a bit at that, and frowned. "In what
way?"

"Well . . ." Edward put his head to the side as he thought,
and Jack realized it was an action all the Carringtons seemed
to copy from Julia. "He's a great gun; but I told you that.
And he goes his own way, and does what he wishes, and is
up to all sorts of larks, and isn't afraid of anything, and all
the ladies swoon over him—"

Edward saw Jack's frown deepen and stopped, saying
self-consciously that perhaps he shouldn't have said that
about the ladies. Jack shrugged and said there was no accounting for ladies' tastes, which made Edward grin as he
waited for the next question. It was not long in coming.

"So with your mother and uncle gone so much of the
time, is there no one else who helps your sister see to the estate and the children?" Jack asked.

Edward said that their neighbor, old Mr. Hartwell, was quite good about helping Julia when she had questions about crops and sheep, and the servants had been with them forever, and were always helping with the little ones. And of course the vicar was always putting a word in. . . .

Jack, who had frowned at the mention of old Mr. Hartwell, wondering how old the gentleman actually was, as seen from Edward's tender years, grinned at the young man's last remark, and the disconsolate tone in which it was uttered.

"Not always a *welcome* word, I take it," the viscount said.

Edward looked shamefaced and said he supposed he shouldn't mind the man so; after all, Julia said the vicar was terribly worthy, and they should all respect his calling, but it was just that he prosed at one in such a pompous way.

Jack nodded in sympathy. "I know the type," he said. "They make you want to run out and do something dastardly, just to show them."

Edward grinned. "And I don't like the way he looks at Julia, either," the young man offered.

"Oh?" Jack's amusement seemed to vanish in the moment, and Edward wondered uneasily what he'd said to make Viscount Chalmsy's brows draw together like that. "How does he look at her, then?"

Edward bit his lip for a moment, trying to put the image into words. At last he shrugged and said, "Oh, I don't know; as if she's the last cake on the tea tray, perhaps, and he's going to have the last cake."

Edward frowned, and Jack sensed it was an issue the boy took quite personally.

"He always does have the last cake, you see," Edward explained, "no matter how many he has already had, and no matter that someone else might not have had any, being late for tea. He seems to think it is his right, because he's the vicar."

"I see." Jack nodded, his brow dark. "You don't like the man much, do you?"

Edward flushed, and said that Julia told them it was wrong to dislike a man of the cloth. He seemed relieved when Jack said he couldn't see the sense in that; men of the cloth could be just as disagreeable as the next fellow. Edward leaned forward and, after glancing around for a moment, as if to be sure no one else could hear him, said in a lowered voice that he rather thought so, too.

He added that none of the younger Carringtons liked the man, and added with pardonable disgust, "Why, he gave us all a catechism for Christmas last year—and then actually expected us to have read it when next he visited!" Jack said the man was not to be believed, which met with Edward's complete approval.

The viscount's inquiries as to other family members—aunts and uncles—who might care for the Carringtons brought answers that made his brow furrow; it was apparent several of Mrs. Carrington's sisters were well connected, but no one had made a real push to help the Carrington children after their father's demise.

Something Edward said in passing suggested to the viscount that while the young man didn't realize it, Mrs. Carrington's family felt the lady had married beneath them when she attached herself to a younger son. As Edward talked the viscount realized that both the late Mr. Carrington and the absent Uncle William were younger sons in a family where the eldest brother cared not at all for his siblings. Jack could well imagine that when Mr. Carrington died, no offers of help had come from the head of his family line—a hunch Edward unconsciously confirmed when he said it was too bad his father's oldest brother wasn't as good-hearted as Uncle William.

"And of course when Papa died Julia didn't get to go up to town for a season," Edward was saying, making Jack realize that he'd been lost in his own thoughts as the young man chatted on. "Not that it mattered, she said—she said she was relieved, really, because she would have missed us all so much, and she was sure she wouldn't take—Papa's great-aunt Julia was to bring her out, but then the old lady died, too, within a year after Papa. Julia was named for her, and Papa always said the old lady had a kindness for Jules."

Edward sat for several moments in silence, his head tilted to the side as he puzzled on something. At last he looked at Jack and said, his voice hesitant, "I don't know why Jules thinks she wouldn't have taken—any man would be a fool not to like her."

The viscount, pleased to see a militant spark grow in Edward's eye as the young man spoke the last words, said, "Quite so." Then he brought Edward back to a question that still troubled him. In the smoothest manner possible Jack turned the topic to ask if the Mr. Hartwell Edward had mentioned earlier was as frequent a visitor as the vicar.

Edward shook his head and said that when Julia wanted Mr. Hartwell's advice she always went to him; the octogenarian seldom left his grounds as a result of an injured leg that had not healed well when he fell from a horse several years ago. In fact, Edward continued chattily, they all went to visit Mr. Hartwell at least once a week; he had been like a grandfather to them ever since Edward could remember.

Jack nodded and agreed that it really was too bad about Mr. Hartwell's leg. He did not question or in any way explore why Edward's information on Mr. Hartwell's age made him feel better.

Chapter
Nine

By the end of the fourth day of Viscount Chalmsy's enforced
bed rest his cold was improving, but his temper was so foul
that Jack could not even stand himself.

He had shouted at John when the groom stoutly refused to
visit the nearest inn and see if there was a conveyance of
some sort that the viscount could use to return to London,
and when the servant went so far as to say that he wouldn't
be doing any such thing until it had Miss Carrington's approval, just as his lordship's brother had instructed, Jack so
far forgot himself as to hurl his shaving mug at his faithful
henchman.

The viscount had not meant to hit his friend, of course,
and did not, but as the mug made a resounding and quite sat-
isfying crashing sound against the wall, Jack realized too
late that it was the only shaving mug he had. The loud expletive that followed that realization made John fold his lips
and nod, as if to say, "There, now, that showed you, didn't it?"

If that wasn't bad enough, the sound of that splendid
crash quickly brought several of the Carringtons to Jack's
room. William and Lily arrived first, and were followed in
short order by Cressida. None of the new arrivals seemed to
comprehend what had happened, even though John by that

time was kneeling on the carpet, recovering the shattered remains of the viscount's mug. Lily, ever worried for the viscount's health, moved forward anxiously to ask Jack if he was quite all right.

Thoroughly disgusted with himself for the scene he had created and in which he was playing such a prominent part, Jack snapped a "Yes." Unfortunately the forcefulness of his tone, far from reassuring the little girl, made her gasp. The situation went from bad to worse as Lily, stricken, took a step back, tears welling in her eyes and running in silence down her cheeks.

William, who up until this point had shown every indication of worshiping the viscount quite as much as his older brother did, abandoned that idea and took up the cudgels in his sister's defense. He castigated the viscount as a "bad man" for making Lily cry, and showed an eloquence Jack had heretofore not noticed in the boy's speech. William said that he hoped they would soon be rid of the viscount, since they didn't need him around to make Lily cry. There were already enough things that did that.

Jack, whose lips had curled up at William's unthinking assessment of his sister's proclivity to tears, quickly schooled them as the boy frowned darkly at him. The viscount tried to apologize but William was having none of it; instead, William put his arm around his younger sister's shoulders and gave her a squeeze, telling her to never mind what that old viscount said, because Julia said he was just a London dandy, didn't she, and who cared what a dandy said, anyway?

Jack, stunned—and more than a little annoyed—at being apostrophized as a dandy, was even more appalled by the little girl's continued tears, and his responsibility for them. He found himself much in agreement with William, calling himself several terms much harsher than "a bad man" as he tried in vain to apologize to Lily.

The little girl could not hear him, however; she was distracted both by William's continued insults on her behalf, and by John's heavy mutterings, which also were directed at the viscount.

The groom, after casting Jack one dark look that made it abundantly clear what *he* thought of his master's behavior, totally ignored Viscount Chalmsy. John knelt beside the little girl and put one arm around her shoulders and one arm around William's as he offered to punch his lordship's lights out for her, if that would make her feel better.

That offer earned the groom a soft chuckle from Lily and instantaneous approval from William, who was adjuring John to make good on the threat. Cressida, whose reproachful glances made the viscount squirm, said in her soft voice that she was sure it was very kind of John to offer, but she did not believe they could have fisticuffs in the house—Julia would not like it—no matter (and here she turned her full and shaming gaze on the hapless Jack) how great the provocation might be.

Viscount Chalmsy was heartily wishing that the floor would open up and swallow him, bed and all, when into the hubbub walked Julia Carrington, demanding in a no-nonsense voice to be told what was happening. Lord Chalmsy's already high color heightened as four excited voices tried at once to explain.

The mingling of their voices and the disjointed way they went about the task made their explanations incomprehensible, but a quick glance around the room, the pained look on the viscount's face, the shards of broken shaving mug and

Lily's tears gave Julia a pretty good idea. Holding up a hand for silence she confounded her audience by looking, not at those clustered around her, so eager to lodge their complaints, but at the man in the bed as she asked, "*What* has happened here?"

Jack took a deep breath and tried to meet her eyes, but found he could not. He turned his focus instead to the end of his bed as he said, in a voice that sounded petulant even to his own ears, "I have behaved very badly, and I am heartily sorry for it."

Julia wanted to laugh aloud at his little-boy face, and the sulky manner in which he hunkered down under the covers, but she kept her own expression schooled to one of polite interest. She wondered to herself when the viscount would learn to think first and snap later, and decided it probably would not be for some time, if it ever did occur. Although Miss Carrington could not help but think that if Viscount Chalmsy was around Lily for any amount of time, he might learn sooner than expected. . . .

Miss Carrington had a pretty good idea of how the viscount was petted and cosseted by society, for John had told her much that morning as she visited with him in the stable. Such societal adoration seldom encouraged the taming of tempers, Miss Carrington knew, and it occurred to her that the proud viscount was learning a bit more about humility than he cared to know during his sojourn at Carrington Place.

None of that showed in her face, however, as Jack took an even deeper breath and tried to smile. Miss Carrington, watching him critically, noted that the effort came off badly.

The viscount continued in a more moderate tone, speaking to the youngest Carrington as if she were the only one in the room. "I am especially sorry that I have injured your feelings, Lily, when I know that it was only goodness on your part that made you ask after my health. I am not used to being so well looked after, you see, and I do not seem to know how to behave in the face of such kindness."

John, who believed the viscount had always been only too well looked after, appeared quite stunned by his master's statement, Julia noted, but it occurred to her that the look of astonishment on the groom's face might be put there as much by the fact that the viscount was making an apology as by the words Jack chose to use. Lily, of course, did not know the magnitude of what was occurring, having never been privy to late-night conversations at White's in London, where more than one of Jack's intimates had heard the viscount say more times than any of them could count, "Never apologize; never explain."

The little girl, who had run to Julia as soon as her eldest sister entered the room, throwing her arms around Miss Carrington's waist and burying her face in Julia's gown, stood now with her sister gently stroking her hair. Jack was relieved when the child, her arms still wrapped tightly around Julia's waist, raised her head and looked cautiously toward him.

"Sometimes," the viscount said, trying his best to ignore the others crowding the room as he spoke only to Lily, "I do not—*think*—before I speak. Or act. It is a fault—a fault whose enormity I do not believe I have ever before considered. I am sure your sister would say it is a grave fault"—here the eldest Miss Carrington smiled, but the viscount did not see it; his eyes were still fixed on the child—"a fault I will try to contain in future. I hope"—he held a hand out coaxingly, and offered a crooked smile—"that you will be able to find it in your heart to forgive me."

Julia, who had continued to stroke her sister's hair through the viscount's speech, felt the little girl's hold on her waist slacken. Lily took a hesitant step forward, then paused, looking back at Julia. Her sister nodded encouragement and at last Lily smiled. Everyone else in the room smiled in reflex, and the viscount heard John and Cressida utter audible sighs.

"Julia," the little girl confided, taking another step forward, "says we really mustn't mind what you say. She says you cannot help taking pets. She says you are spoiled by society and cross because you cannot bear having your will foiled."

That surprised a sound out of John, a sound the groom tried his best to turn into a cough. Jack frowned at him but the groom did not look up, especially when Lord Chalmsy, realizing Lily was waiting expectantly for an answer, agreed in as neutral a tone as he could muster that that could very well be true.

"She says you have never before encountered that—" Lily began.

Miss Carrington, her cheeks redder than they had been a moment earlier, stepped up behind the little girl to say as she wrapped her arms around the child's shoulders, "Yes, well, I know you would like to chat, my dear, but I am sure the viscount is feeling quite in need of a nap now."

The viscount, relieved to have someone else's behavior under consideration, said quite pleasantly that it was no such thing; he was not the least bit sleepy. He invited Lily to seat herself on the edge of his bed and enjoy a comfortable coze, slanting a wicked look up at Julia as he practically purred to the child, "And tell me what else Julia says."

The eldest Miss Carrington, two bright spots of color burning in her cheeks, bodily lifted Lily onto her hip and adjured the little girl to wish the viscount sweet dreams, because in spite of himself he was going to follow doctor's orders and rest, and they were going to help him.

With her usual briskness she bade William and Cressida precede her from the room, and reminded them that they had studies to attend to. She walked quickly toward the door, still carrying Lily, who waved at Jack over her sister's shoulder—a wave he returned with a gentle smile John could not remember having seen on the viscount's face before.

The groom saw the smile grow when Miss Carrington paused a moment at the door and half turned. She cradled Lily's face to her shoulder and the little girl did not see the look of reproach Miss Carrington directed at the viscount before disappearing from sight.

John's lips pursed in silent speculation as a chuckle broke from the viscount when the door was safely latched behind Julia. The groom, who had formed a favorable impression of Miss Carrington the moment he saw how she had cared for the viscount's horses, was smiling to himself as he set about the task of cleaning up the remains of Jack's temper tantrum.

Chapter
Ten

On the sixth day, Dr. Smythley pronounced the viscount well enough to move about Carrington Place with the use of a cane and "his lordship's good judgment." Miss Carrington, who was present for that pronouncement, could not be sure if it came because of the doctor's assessment of Lord Chalmsy's health, or because of the viscount's forceful assertion that if the doctor did not assure Miss Carrington that it would be quite all right for him to be up and about, said viscount would forcefully pitch said doctor out the window. She also could not help but notice how John rolled his eyes at Dr. Smythley's reference to the viscount's good judgment.

Trying not to laugh, Julia bit her lip and concentrated for a moment on the vicar's last sermon, a sure remedy against levity of any sort. When she thought she had herself in hand she glanced up to find the viscount frowning broodingly, first at his groom, then at his hostess. In spite of herself she grinned.

"Perhaps," Dr. Smythley said, clearing his throat in the nervous and excessively irritating manner he had, a manner made even more nervous by the way the viscount was glaring at him, "Miss Carrington will be able to find you a cane."

The doctor took a cautious step nearer the door and farther away from the window, an action that brought a chilling smile to the viscount's lips.

Miss Carrington, seeing Dr. Smythley gulp, took pity on the man. She said that she would do so immediately, and escorted the doctor from the room, thoughtfully fortifying him with tea and scones before sending him on to his next patient. The viscount, who in his few days with her had come to know the lady to be as good as her word—in fact, it occurred to him, he had come to depend on it—ordered John to help him into the best of the meager possessions Phipps had brought him the day the valet gave his notice, and waited. Within half an hour Edward appeared at the viscount's door bearing an exceedingly handsome ebony cane topped with an intricately carved lion's head. It had been their grandfather's, the young man explained, and Julia said that the viscount was to use it, and if his lordship cared to do so, Edward was to help him down the stairs to the library, or the morning room, whichever the viscount preferred. Unless his lordship wished to remain in his room, which would certainly be understandable.

Jack, who rejected the idea of remaining in his room another day—even another minute—with every sign of loathing, took the cane and hobbled several steps, leaning heavily on it when his injured ankle proclaimed its unwillingness to carry the full weight the viscount tried to put on it. His sharp frown and the way his jaws clamped together, as if to stifle an exclamation, made John say that perhaps just walking about the room for a little bit might not be a bad idea.

The viscount assured him it was. It was a very bad idea. Lord Chalmsy also was firm in his refusal to accept Edward's offer of a strong shoulder to lean on as he made his way downstairs; a refusal that earned him a protest from his groom. It was a protest he ignored.

A fine figure he would look, Jack said, not even able to get himself down the stairs! John, with concern in his eyes, said roughly that it wasn't looks he should be concerned with, just now, and as for that, he didn't imagine there was anybody in the house for the viscount to impress, them already having drawn their own conclusions about him. The servant noticed that Lord Chalmsy's color heightened a bit at that but the viscount remained firm; Edward might show him the way,—to the library, he decided—but Jack would arrive under his own power.

He did, too, but by the time his lordship stood in the main hall of Carrington Place he was sweating heavily, and muttering that he didn't know what business people had putting so many stairs in their houses, anyway.

Miss Carrington, dressed in a simple green gown that reminded the viscount of spring, was coming down the hall when he stepped off the last stair, and she stopped in surprise at the sight of him. Without thinking she asked Edward why he hadn't helped the viscount, when it was so clear walking gave him difficulty.

John, who had taken the steps one by one behind his master, ready to catch the viscount should he start to fall, informed the hall at large that there were those wise enough to offer to help, but not always those wise enough to accept. Julia, seeing the confusion on Edward's face and the glare on the viscount's, said that yes, well, that was done now, and perhaps the viscount would care to sit down?

Jack, who wanted to do so above everything, refused instantly, and told her through clenched teeth that he much preferred to stand. At her look of clear disbelief, he added that it was good to be on his feet again. There was no reason, he said, for them to have kept him tied to his bed for so long.

The words were forcefully uttered, but their effect was somewhat spoiled by the unfortunate way the viscount swayed just after he uttered them. Miss Carrington, much more a born commander than her brother, moved at once to Jack's side and, slapping his hand when he tried to pull it out of her grasp, adjured him not to be a total nodcock. For good measure she added that he must stop acting like a stubborn child at once.

John, grinning at the look of astonishment that crossed the viscount's face, hastily wiped the expression from his lips as Lord Chalmsy looked back toward him, almost as if for help.

"Come along, do," Miss Carrington said, ignoring the viscount's surprise. "There's no reason for you to be in pain when we can make you more comfortable. I assure you no one here will think the less of you for choosing sense over swagger!"

"*Over swag—*" The viscount, who was allowing himself to be moved toward the library, leaning as much as he could on his cane and more thankfully than he cared to admit on the capable Miss Carrington, stopped and looked down at her in astonishment.

She, glancing up, met his eyes, and her own grew rueful. "Oh, dear," she said, "you're not going to ask me if I know who I'm talking to again, are you?"

The way the viscount stiffened told her it was a poor reference for the moment, and she bit her lip. "And now I've done it, haven't I?"

Lord Chalmsy, who by this time was moving forward

again, disengaged his arm from her shoulders by the simple
expedient of falling gratefully into the first chair inside the
library door. Then he looked up and said, in the tones of one
much goaded, that he had no idea what she was talking
about.

Miss Carrington laughed. "Oh, no!" she said. "That's why
you pokered up on me just now."

The viscount said instantly that he had done no such
thing, for he never "pokered." Before she could respond he
turned pointedly away from her, and ordered John to bring
him the small stool he had spotted by the fireplace.

Miss Carrington stayed the groom by putting a hand on
his arm. In a reasonable voice she asked the viscount if he
wouldn't rather actually sit by the fire? There was a chill in
the air, and he could see out the windows from the big wing
chairs near the mantel.

"I am perfectly comfortable, I assure you!" snapped the
viscount, who was anything but on the small wooden chair
he'd chosen for expediency.

Miss Carrington nodded, her eyes brimming with mis-
chief and her lips pursed in a way that showed Lord
Chalmsy how little she believed him.

"Well—" She turned away from the viscount and toward
John, rolling her eyes; Jack saw the groom's slight nod and
frowned in suspicion. "Edward and I will just be going
then," the lady said, moving out the door. "We'll have a light
luncheon sent in shortly—unless you'd care to return to
your room before you eat?"

Jack made short and ungracious shrift of that suggestion,
then watched as the door closed behind the brother and sister. When he and his groom were alone he sat for several
moments, frowning up at the man before he snapped, in the

tones of one pushed beyond endurance, "Oh, very well, then! Help me to that chair by the fire, and not a word! Not a word, I tell you!"

John, following his employer's instructions to the letter, vouchsafed not a syllable as he leaned down and pulled one of the viscount's arms around his shoulders. The groom heaved his injured master out of the chair and helped him toward the fireplace, where he gently settled him into a comfortable old chair and tucked a stool under the viscount's ailing ankle.

Not a word did he speak. But his eyes said volumes.

Jack was joined within the hour by William, Lily, Cressida, and Edward. They were proceeded into the room by the elderly family butler, who busied himself pulling a small table from its place near the wall and placing it at the viscount's right hand. Edward helped, then set four chairs around the table as the housekeeper entered with a tray bearing dishes, cutlery and linens. When she'd arranged those to her liking she withdrew and returned in short order with a large tureen of soup and a basket of still-warm bread, which she bade them all eat up while it was hot. Beaming upon them in a way that reminded Jack of his favorite governess, she bobbed a curtsy and withdrew, leaving Jack with his young hosts and hostesses. When Cressida reached for the large spoon in the tureen and began ladling the soup into their bowls, Jack asked if the eldest Miss Carrington wouldn't be joining them. Cressida smiled.

"No, my lord," Cressida said in her soft voice. "Julia has ridden over to visit Mr. Hartwell. She does so every week, and she asked me to excuse her absence to you, although she said . . ." Cressida paused to ponder Julia's words, tucking a stray strand of silky blond hair back behind her ear as her blue eyes smiled at the viscount. She really was a most amazingly beautiful girl, Jack thought. "She said she doubted you would mind her absence too much, my lord. I didn't quite understand that. Do you?"

Edward, who had taken a spoonful of soup just as his sister made her artless disclosure, choked and had to be pounded on the back by William, who undertook the task with enthusiasm. As soon as he had convinced his younger brother to leave off beating him, Edward said that Cressida must have misunderstood; he was sure Julia had said she *hoped* the viscount would not much mind her absence. When Cressida seemed inclined to argue the point a harrassed Edward turned the topic by reporting that Lord Chalmsy's horses were healing by the day; in fact, John said they would soon be ready to drive.

"Well—" Jack grimaced down at his ankle, which was throbbing more than he wished to acknowledge. He thought morosely that it sounded as if his animals were doing better than he was. "That's certainly good news. Then I won't be a burden to you much longer."

He was startled—even gratified—to find four pairs of fine Carrington eyes suddenly turned upon him in varying shades of surprise.

"You're not going away, are you?" Lily asked, her soup forgotten as she raised anxious eyes to Lord Chalmsy.

"Well, you do understand that I'm only a visitor here," Jack started, saw her face begin to cloud, and added hastily, "of course, I won't be leaving for several days, I'm sure; until my ankle is healed well enough."

The sun came out on Lily's face and Jack, relieved, did not notice the thoughtful glances that passed between Cressida and Edward. The viscount, in a move that would have astonished his family and all those who knew him in London, asked Lily and William how they had spent their morning, and evinced much interest in the new kittens in the stable loft. He promised to hobble down and examine what he was assured was a most noble brood as soon as he was able.

The viscount had returned to his room by the time Julia Carrington arrived back at Carrington Place that afternoon. He told John—much to John's surprise—that his exertion had worn him out more than he liked to admit.

Julia, looking in to see if there might be anything Lord Chalmsy needed, saw that he was asleep, and tiptoed forward to quietly tuck the cover up around his shoulder, just as she would have for William and Lily. She stood for a moment looking down at him, and smiled at the way an unruly lock of hair had fallen forward onto his forehead in his sleep. It made him look younger, and vulnerable. That vulnerability was not apparent when he was awake, disguised as it was by the arrogant manner in which the man carried himself and the aristocratic way he had of looking down his nose to quash pretension.

She was just turning to go when his eyes, clouded with sleep, opened, and he stared in puzzlement up toward her for a moment. "Julia?" he said, his voice heavy with sleep.

Miss Carrington smiled. "Shhh!" she said, not resisting the urge to reach down and push the lock of hair gently back from his forehead. "You're dreaming!"

The viscount, so assured, closed his eyes and again lapsed into heavy sleep, where he did dream—repeatedly—of Julia Carrington.

Chapter
Eleven

Julia Carrington sat that night before her dressing table, slowly sliding the brush again and again through her heavy chestnut-colored hair. She stared for a long moment at the face that had been staring back at her for twenty-four years now, noting the brown eyes, the high forehead, the generous lips that quirked up even as she gazed at herself. Slowly her brush hand stilled.

What was she looking for, anyway?

Beauty?

Julia's lips turned up even more. She had only to look at her sister Cressida to know that the world would never proclaim Julia Carrington a great beauty.

What she had in her face was humor; intelligence, Mr. Hartwell said, compassion and common sense. . . .

Julia sighed. Nothing she had ever heard suggested that men such as Viscount Chalmsy were drawn to humor, intelligence and common sense—not that it mattered! Not at all!

Resolutely she began to briskly brush her hair again. It was foolish to even think of such things. Viscount Chalmsy was their guest; a man who, through misfortune, had come into their home, and would leave it again as soon as he was able. Had she met him in London—had her season occurred, had her father not died, and then Father's great-aunt Julia—Miss Carrington had no doubts that had they met at any social event, Viscount Chalmsy would have looked right past the little country miss with the turned-up nose and the regrettable tendency to laugh at life's foibles.

They were so very different.

And yet . . .

Once again Julia's brush hand slowed. He was spoiled and stubborn, strong-willed, easily irritated, and excessively irritating.

And yet . . .

There was something about him. Something she could like a great deal, if she was not careful.

His concern for the children as he lay in the ditch that first night, when they brought him to Carrington Place—that had pleased her. His kindness to Lily—to all the children, really. It all suggested a good-heartedness at odds with his carefully cultivated insouciant image.

He had shown remarkable tolerance with Edward, for Miss Carrington was sure her brother's eager questions about London life must bore the viscount considerably. And he had *not* fallen in love with Cressida, or flirted outrageously with her, which was a relief to Julia, who wasn't at all sure how her country-bred sister would react to the practiced compliments of a known rake. In fact, Viscount Chalmsy now treated Cressie in an avuncular way that made Miss Carrington smile when she pictured how unbelieving his London friends would be of such behavior in the presence of a young lovely.

He had been concerned for Julia, too, when he asked about her mother and uncle. She did not *need* his concern, of course, for she was perfectly able to handle her family's affairs—had been doing so for some time now. But his interest had touched her.

Not since her father had died had anyone really seemed to understand that perhaps even the self-sufficient and capable Miss Carrington might like, every now and then, to have someone else take the lead, or bear the bigger part of a burden.

Julia grinned at herself in the mirror. This was silly, she knew. The viscount had come, the viscount would leave and life at Carrington Place would go on as it always had. And that was that.

With a resolute nod at her mirror image she replaced her brush on her neat dressing table and started to turn. As she did so she could almost swear the reflection in the mirror whispered, "But there will be memories, and memories can warm cold winters to come."

Miss Carrington, not of a fanciful nature, looked quickly back. She stared for a long moment into wide brown eyes. At last she sighed.

"Papa used to say it is a wise person who knows how to enjoy each day," she told her reflection, the words coming out low, and slow. "So perhaps it would be . . . wise . . . to enjoy what we can."

Gravely the woman in the mirror nodded. Julia stared at her for some time before she at last rose, and went thoughtfully to bed.

One week had slipped into two, and the second into a third, when Miss Carrington reluctantly broached the topic of his leaving with the viscount. They were sitting in the garden at the time, watching Lily and William play with the puppy Edward had found abandoned on one of his rides about the neighborhood, and had brought home. The children were running this way and that, shouting with pleasure as the puppy bounded after first one, then the other of them. Jack was torn between watching the children and watching Julia Carrington watching them, for he enjoyed the way her face lit up at sight of their joy. Jack smiled when she turned to him suddenly, as if she felt his gaze upon her. Her own eyes held a question, and Jack smiled again.

"They are wonderful children," he told her.

Julia nodded. "I am so grateful they are healthy and happy," she said. "When William was a baby he was forever taking colds, and the poor child would cough so it wrung my heart to hear him, but he seems to have outgrown that now. And Lily—" Her eyes returned to the little girl who had collapsed upon the ground with the puppy on top of her, and was lying in a pile of petticoats and giggles. "Lily almost died when she was one, and I was so afraid—"

She stopped suddenly and blushed, her gaze returning to his as she said, "I am so sorry! I start talking about the children, and it seems I never stop! I know you can have no interest in children's diseases."

"No!" Without thinking, Jack leaned forward and touched her wrist, his face serious as he said, "I am very interested. Really. They are fine children; I have grown quite fond of them in my time here. And I am always interested in what interests you—"

He wished the last words unsaid as soon as they were out of his mouth, for Miss Carrington, whose attention had been fixed upon his strong fingers as they rested on her skin, raised suddenly startled eyes to his and shifted in her chair. She looked away as she moved her body away from him, and Jack, puzzled by what he had perceived as pain in her eyes, was even more surprised by her next words.

"Yes, well—" The normally calm Miss Carrington was flustered, and she did not like that one bit. "The children have grown very fond of you, too—in fact, so fond that—well, they are children, after all, and children tend to assume that the world will go on forever as it goes on now, so they don't realize they must guard their hearts. That is—"

The way Julia's hand flew to her suddenly hot cheeks told the viscount that she had not meant to say that, and he frowned at the words.

"Guard their hearts, Miss Carrington?"

He repeated the words, which hung like so many icicles on stone between them.

Julia took a deep breath and smiled tightly as she said, "They will miss you very much when you go away, my lord. And every day you stay means they will miss you that much more. Even though they know in their heads that you are only with us temporarily—heaven knows I have told them that often enough!—in their hearts they seem to think—that is—"

She turned her head away, and once again looked out over the garden. Lily, William, and the puppy had wandered down to the small pond at the edge of the lawn, and Julia called a warning to them to keep themselves and the puppy from falling in. Then she squared her shoulders and once again turned to face the frowning viscount.

"Would it be so terrible if I remained forever in their hearts?" he demanded. He wanted to ask, "And what about your heart, Julia Carrington?" but he left the words unsaid.

It was, he thought, too soon.

Too soon to tell her that in the time they'd spent together

in the last few weeks he'd come to anticipate their verbal duels; too soon to tell her how he looked forward to the hour she put aside for him each afternoon, to keep him company, offering a game of chess, or conversation on the days she brought her never-ending mending with her. Too soon to tell her he enjoyed the stories she told the children each evening every bit as much as Lily and William did.

It was too soon, he felt, to tell her that he rather liked her managing ways—on second thought, he wasn't sure he'd ever tell her that—and the concern she showed when he or the children did not eat their dinner.

She had confided to him her wishes that Cressida could have a season, and that Edward might get to travel as he wished to do, and that someone he admired would take the young man in hand and impress upon him the importance of continuing his schooling. The viscount was waiting for her to realize he might help with those wishes. If he went away now, he was sure she would never realize it.

He thought for a moment of how his sister-in-law, Arabella, would laugh, to find that her brother-in-law, immune to all the lures thrown at him by the ton's diamonds of the first water, had succumbed to a pair of fine brown eyes and full lips much more likely to be bent on scolding than enticing him.

No, Jack thought. He would not have it. He would not go away, no matter what Julia said. It was too soon. Too soon to tell her he didn't know how it had happened, but he'd gone from wanting to avoid leg shackling at all costs to wanting to take on a ready-made family—as long as Julia Carrington, with her calm outlook on life and her kindness and her lively sense of the ridiculous, was the key to that family. So he said again, preparing to fight, "Would it be so terrible, then?"

"Of course not!" Julia shook her head, distressed that he had misunderstood her. "But you have healed quite well now, and will be returning to your world, and they will remain here—we all will remain here. . . ."

The words trailed off, and for a moment Jack thought her voice had quavered, but it was quite steady when she spoke again. "I know you never wanted to be here, my lord, and we are all so sorry for the accident that befell you. You have in the last week been quite gracious about your enforced recuperation, but I know—you said at the beginning—that you are anxious to return to London, so I have taken the liberty of writing to your brother to inform him that the doctor says you are well enough to travel, and that if he should care to come for you—at his convenience, of course!—I am sure you will be quite ready to return to your family and your London life. . . ."

Her words ended uncertainly as she stared at Jack. The viscount, who had never been gracious in his life, was struggling with that definition of his behavior and his indignation that Dr. Smythley, whom he had paid quite handsomely to say that the viscount was recovering even slower than the good doctor—who had made no quick-recovery diagnosis— had expected, and that Jack would need to stay at least another week to be sure all his injuries were healed, had not held to their bargain.

The viscount, who had the first day he awoke in the bedroom assigned him in the Carrington home thought he could not leave fast enough, had found, in the last two weeks, that he had little inclination to leave at all. Now the reason for his turnabout in attitude calmly sat telling him that she had written his family and asked that they remove him—at their convenience, she said, but Jack understood that to mean as soon as possible—and that was thwarting the plan he was trying to put into action.

Jack did not like to have his plans thwarted. He did not like it at all.

"My lord?"

The viscount realized Miss Carrington was looking at him questioningly just as he realized his mouth was hanging open, and he closed his jaws with a snap.

"Well!" he said. "I did not realize my presence here was so repugnant to you that you could not *wait* to be rid of me!"

"Repug—" Julia started to repeat the word, as if stunned, then shook her head, as if to clear it.

"Oh, no," she said, holding out one hand almost beseechingly. "Your presence here—well, after the first week, anyway!—has been *far* from repugnant! But it cannot go on, so it is best that it end before the pain that ending causes grows any greater."

Jack, pleased to hear his leaving would cause pain in the Carrington household, and prideful enough to hope Miss Carrington would feel at least part of that pain herself, smiled at her allusion to the behavior of his first week with them. Suddenly he said, with far less finesse than he was known for, "Well, why can't it go on?"

Miss Carrington put another hand out, almost as if to ward him off, which astounded the viscount, who had not moved. The lady rose and took a step away from him as she said, not looking at him, "You jest, I know, and you should not."

She pasted a smile on her face as the children approached, the puppy running circles around them as they came. Quietly she said, so only Jack could hear her, "I have had a reply from your family, and although it was vaguely worded, I believe someone will be here tomorrow to collect you. I will tell the children tonight, before dinner. I hope you will make it as easy as you can for them."

Jack, who wanted to shout and stamp his feet and throw things while he demanded to be told just who was to make it easy for him, rose and bowed stiffly. His eyes glittered with anger, and his jaw was so tight it made it difficult to force the words through as he said, "Of course."

He turned and, stabbing his cane viciously down with each step, made his way into the house. Julia, watching him go, said "My lord?" in an uncertain voice, but when he paused she said no more.

Not looking back, the viscount moved on, slamming the door behind him as he entered the house. He slammed every door he could find on his way up to his room and, not feeling the least relieved, slammed *that* door three times, giving it a kick for good measure and regretting that action immediately, for he'd used his injured foot.

Swearing a blue streak, the viscount hobbled over to the bed and flung himself down upon it, propping his foot up on a pillow and putting his hands behind his head, the better to stare at the ceiling. His frown never left his face until John came to help him dress for supper.

William and Lily, watching him stalk away from their sister, tilted their heads consideringly for a moment, then gazed knowledgeably up at her.

"Taken another pet, has he?" Lily asked, smiling trustingly at Julia. Miss Carrington, smiling despite the ache in her throat, reached out and smoothed back the hair that had come loose from Lily's braid.

"Yes, dear," Julia said, bending to hug her sister to her with an intensity that surprised and slightly worried the sensitive Lily. "He has taken another pet."

There was a moment of silence as Lily and William exchanged glances. Julia gave herself a shake and, dropping an arm around William's shoulders, too, said, with a smile, "And speaking of pets, what say we go find a treat for this one? Perhaps a bone for Sir Lancelot (for so Lily had christened the pup), and a cherry tart or two for his friends?"

The children, thinking that a fine idea, raced toward the kitchen, Sir Lancelot at their heels. They were not aware that as their sister followed them at a more decorous pace she stopped, several times, to look back toward the pleasant garden, and once, to look up, at a window at which no face appeared.

Chapter
Twelve

Dinner that night was strained.

Jack, who had never before been asked to leave any home he was a guest in—who was, in fact, much more used to hostesses begging him to stay a few more days, to grace their gatherings—came dangerously close to pouting, his face when he first joined the family in the cheery if threadbare drawing room a morose mask.

When he stalked stiffly toward them it was readily apparent that Miss Carrington, always as good as her word, had announced his imminent departure. Lily's eyes were red rimmed, and William looked rebellious. Edward and Cressida sat talking quietly, their faces uncharacteristically sober, and they both eyed him with considerable speculation when he entered. Julia Carrington obviously had just finished mopping her youngest sibling's eyes and was holding a wet handkerchief when she became aware of the viscount, frowning heavily at her as he stood in the doorway, filling the space with his tall frame and wide shoulders.

He was such an imposing-looking man, she thought; no wonder all the ladies in London . . . Julia turned her attention to Lily; it did her no good to think about how all the ladies in London tried to attract the viscount's attention. One day, Julia was sure, the Carringtons would hear of his approaching nuptials, and she was sure they would all wish him well—they *would*—

Suddenly aware of the way she was twisting and pulling the handkerchief through her fingers, Julia stopped and stuffed the small scrap of linen and lace into her sleeve. She glanced up to find the viscount broodingly regarding her.

He was wondering what it was that had so greatly exercised her, but he had little time to consider it; as soon as Lily saw him she launched herself from her chair and ran toward him, throwing her arms around his waist and holding tight as she implored him not to go.

The viscount, much discomposed, almost lost his balance and had to put a hand out against the wall to steady himself. With the other hand he patted the child's head and tried to think of comforting things to say. Since none came to him, he settled on "There, there!" and cast Miss Carrington a look of defiance that clearly said, "Now see what you've done!"

Julia started forward but it was Edward who actually rescued the viscount, lifting his little sister into his arms and saying, in a tone that fluctuated between bracing and teasing, "Now, now, Lily! You don't want to be crying all over the viscount's coat! It's much too fine for that! We all knew he was only here for a visit, while he and his horses healed up, didn't we? I'm sure he won't be forgetting you, no matter where he goes! Be a good girl, now, and quit your crying. You're embarrassing us all, you know. We Carringtons have more bottom than that, don't we?"

Viscount Chalmsy thought the words rather harsh for one so young. but they seemed to work. Lily, her arms twined around her brother's neck, gave a watery sniff and nodded into his shoulder as she offered up a soft "I'm sorry." Then she turned her head to ask, with a look that tore at Jack's heart, "*Will* you forget me, my lord?"

"Not ever, Lily," the viscount replied, stepping forward until he could cup the back of the child's head as she rested in Edward's arms. He smiled at her, and then at the young man who held her. "I can promise," the viscount said, looking straight at Julia, "that I will never forget any of you. Ever."

Cressida, watching him and the swift flicker of emotion that played across Julia's face before it was replaced by her sister's most studied calm, pursed her lips and nodded ever so slightly at Edward. Her brother nodded back, and put his youngest sister down onto her feet.

"Well, then," Edward said. "Make the gentleman your best curtsy, Lily, and see if he'll escort you in to dinner. For I don't mind telling you, I'm so hungry I'm going to have to take that bone away from Sir Lancelot if I'm not fed soon!"

The puppy gnawing contentedly in front of the fire raised his head and thumped his tail at mention of his name, and the awkwardness of the moment passed. Lily, with a grace rare in one so young, sank into her best curtsy and, when she rose, tenderly took the arm the viscount held out to her and walked into the dining room at his side. She insisted on sitting at his right hand and William hastily slipped into the chair at the viscount's left. The way the boy's chin thrust out suggested to his family that it would be best to let him remain there.

Julia occupied the chair at the opposite end of the table from the viscount's, and Edward and Cressida sat at her left and right, where they made quite praiseworthy efforts to carry on a conversation through what was a delicious meal that everyone ate but no one tasted.

Julia, whenever she raised her eyes from her food, found the viscount's brooding gaze and the reproachful eyes of her youngest sister and brother upon her—a situation that caused her to take an inordinate interest in her plate. Cressida and Edward directed any number of questions about London and his life there to the viscount, and did not appear in any way put off by his monosyllabic replies, sometimes going so far as to say, "Well, isn't that interesting?" after a brief "yes" or "no" answer.

Lily and William toyed with the food set before them, and for once their eldest sister did not exhort them to eat. How could she, when she seemed to be toying with her food, as well?

When the meal was finally over Jack asked if he might have a moment of Miss Carrington's time but the lady, after casting only the briefest of glances at his tight-lipped visage, decided she had borne enough for one day. She refused him with, "I do not think—that is, the children—I must tuck the children into bed—"

Cressida's offer to do that was firmly refused and, with more haste than dignity, Julia led William and Lily up the stairs, not looking back, as the children did, to say good night. The viscount, watching her go, visibly gnashed his teeth, and Edward cleared his throat.

"My lord," Edward said. "I wonder if Cressida and I might have a word with you."

Jack hunched an impatient shoulder and turned to look at the two. About to decline the request in favor of making serious inroads into the brandy Miss Carrington's butler had taken to leaving on the sideboard in the library for him, he read a refusal to take no for an answer in their eyes and paused. There was an air of suppressed excitement about them; it was as if they were about to embark on a secret mission, and they were smiling at him in such a way. . . .

"Oh, very well!" Jack said ungraciously. "But in the library. And hurry."

Jack sat in the library a half hour later, his second helping of brandy in his hand. He stared accusingly at it, and then at the two young people sitting across from him. They were smiling so expectantly at him that he thought he could not have heard them right, and he shook his head in an effort to clear it, putting the brandy down on the table beside him as he looked first from Cressida to Edward, then back again.

"I beg your pardon?" he said.

Edward moved forward in his chair, and his hands clasped his knees as he spoke, glancing sideways at his sister, who was looking celestial in a gown of robin's egg blue. "Well, Cressida is under the impression . . ." he hedged.

Jack shook his head and actually thumped his palm against his forehead several times before again looking at Edward. "Did you just ask me to marry your sister?" he asked.

Edward looked at Cressida for support, and this time his face contained a considerable amount of uncertainty. "Well," Edward said. "We thought—that is, we hoped—that is—Cressida says . . ."

Jack looked toward the stunning beauty smiling so beatifically at him. His eyebrow rose. "Cressida says?" he repeated, in a dry tone that had been known to make much more sophisticated people than these two think of something else they wished to do in some other place. In a hurry.

Cressida continued to smile at him.

"Cressida says that you are in love with Julia," the beauty

told him, her soft voice almost covered by the snap and crackle of the fire. "I wasn't sure you knew it, but now I am, and so—we thought that we should tell you we think it would be a very good idea if you were to marry Julia."

"You do?" Jack shook his head again, and picked up the brandy. He looked at the nodding Cressida and Edward, and downed the contents.

"Before the vicar offers," Edward said.

Jack frowned.

"The vicar?" He had met that extremely unctuous man three days previously, and the thought of him—or anyone else, for that matter—walking out with Miss Carrington, touching her hair, taking her into his arms . . .

There was a snapping sound, and Jack looked down to find he'd broken the stem of the goblet he held. An oath escaped him as he saw blood well up on his thumb, an oath he quickly apologized for as Cressida moved quickly to pad her handkerchief over the cut, and to take the broken glass from him.

"We don't like the idea either," she said with satisfaction, nodding as the color rose in Jack's cheeks.

"And there really isn't anyone else," Edward said, repeating part of the conversation he and his sister had had earlier. Cressida frowned at him, feeling the viscount might not appreciate that sentiment, but Jack smiled. Edward realized too late that it might have been an infelicitous remark and added hastily that they would, of course, be honored to welcome Lord Chalmsy to the family, because he was, after all, Lord Chalmsy, and any number of women had set their caps for him over the years, and he was top drawer, and so rich—

"Edward." Cressida said the word reproachfully and shook her head at her brother before turning to the viscount.

"You must not think, my lord, that we are after your money," she said. "For while I am sure it is very nice to be rich, it has never been the abiding passion of our lives. Which is a very good thing, I think, because we are not. Rich, that is." She was looking at him so expectantly that Jack felt he should nod, which he did. Cressida appeared satisfied as she went on. "We simply want Julia to be happy, and you seem to make her happy. I don't know why. . . ."

She was standing with her head tilted to the side, as if pondering the question deeply, and it was now her brother's turn to appear shocked. "Cressy, really!" Edward said. His sister seemed surprised.

"Well, I know he is very handsome," she said, speaking to her brother as if the viscount were not in the room—something, Jack thought with a frown, all the Carringtons had a habit of doing—"but that would not argue with Julia. And he is so very bad tempered, forever up in the boughs if his will is crossed. *I* certainly would not want such a bad-tempered man! But there—" She smiled beatifically at them both. "There is no accounting for taste, is there?"

Jack, who had just poured himself more brandy and taken a sip, choked, and had to be pounded on his back by Edward before he could reply, in a stiff voice that made Cressida say wisely that she'd put his back up, that there were any number of young women who found him quite charming, but he was not a marrying man.

"Oh?" Cressida appeared quite surprised by that statement. "Whyever not?"

Jack blinked at her, but his attention was drawn by Edward, who frowned suddenly and said, "Well, if it isn't marriage you've been meaning as you flirted with Julia, and you're not upset about being sent away because you love her, then what?"

The young man's frown deepened and he rose from his chair to stand threateningly over the viscount. "If you have just been trifling with my sister," Edward began, his hands balling at his sides.

Jack, who knew he could knock Edward down without even breathing hard, waved a weary hand and, after taking another gulp of brandy, said, "Oh, do sit down, Galahad. I haven't been trifling. And I haven't been flirting, either! And why you should think a confirmed bachelor such as myself would even contemplate marriage, I would like to know! Why, I think your sister is the most exasperating, strong-willed, opinionated chit I have ever encountered. She doesn't have half the beauty of Cressida sitting there"—he gestured toward the lovely blond, who smiled kindly at him—"and I like beauty. She has a way of taking a man up on everything he says, challenging it and making him look like a fool when he is one—and men don't like that, let me tell you! *I* don't like that! I've never encountered it, except with my exasperating sister-in-law, which doesn't count!

"Julia's challenging, and argumentative, and she doesn't give way just to please me. I have a reputation for having a wicked temper, but does she fear me? Oh, no—she baits me, for goodness' sake! I can't imagine a single reason why I should love her—except that she makes me laugh. And she has such courage as she encounters the world, and she has a way of making a person feel safe, and comfortable, and contented. And her eyes—a man could get lost in her eyes and live there forever. And she is sending me away. Tomorrow."

The viscount tilted the last of his brandy down his throat, and set the glass down with a thud. He looked at it for a long time before he raised his eyes to the two watching him quite intently now, and he smiled a crooked grin. "I have been trying all afternoon to think of a way to stay. Can you help me?"

Neither Edward nor Cressida had any idea of the effort it took for Jack to ask for their help; he could not remember the last time he had told anyone he needed them, and here he was saying the words to two young people he had known only a few weeks. The two did not seem to think any less of him for his admission, however. They seemed to take it so for granted that it occurred to Jack that as family they were used to helping one another.

The viscount thought of how his grandfather and Charles had always been there for him, whenever he had a need, but he had never really *asked* for their help, he had just taken it. He had not said thank you, either—he had held them away, at times, convincing himself that he did not need others, although he liked to think that they needed him. His throat tightened at the thought, and it occurred to him he had some thank-yous to say to those who loved him. And soon.

Edward and Cressida had grown up believing it was the way of things, that people helped people because there was so much need. Their sister had taught them that, by example. Now they were ready to help him.

Edward's suggestion that he just ask Julia to marry him made the viscount nod; he had considered it himself, he told them, but he hadn't been sure how she would react.

When Cressida vetoed that suggestion with a scorn that made her brother glare at her, the viscount sighed and added he'd been afraid it was too soon. Cressida agreed, and said Julia would not have the viscount now. She was sure of it.

"Well, why not, Miss Know-Everything?" Edward demanded, stung to have what he considered the plainest solution refused. "You're the one who said Julia loves him."

"She does?" the viscount interrupted, so hopefully that Cressida took pity on him. Ignoring her brother's obvious desire to fight, she patted the viscount's hand and said that of course Julia loved him, but she hadn't fully allowed herself to realize it yet. Or if she had, she saw only the problems of loving him, and not the joys.

"Problems?" Edward was looking at his sister as if she'd lost her mind. "What problems?"

"Well," Cressida said, wondering how men could be so dense, "there's us, for instance."

"Us?" Edward seemed so surprised that his sister rolled her eyes. She was about to comment on his stupidity when she saw the viscount was looking just as surprised. She sighed.

"Julia," she said, as if talking to two very backward children, "would never ask someone like the viscount to shoulder all of her family. She would never leave us to marry, because she sees us as her responsibility, and she would never ask a man to assume all of us as an instant family, so she really has not thought of wedding—or she has put marriage out of her mind as something that cannot be. Then too, she realizes what society would say about the viscount offering for a mere country miss—"

"What would society say?" Edward asked, taking up the cudgels on his sister's behalf. "Julia is worth half a dozen viscounts, any day!"

"Well, of course she is, stupid," Cressida said, and the viscount again had the sensation of being talked about as if he weren't there. "But society won't think so! They'll say he was trapped into marriage, and—"

"—and Julia could not bear to have people think she trapped me." Jack nodded. "Her integrity is one of the things I most admire about your sister, you know. But it can be quite wearing, too."

Cressida nodded in sympathy, and Edward grumbled that she was very good at throwing cold water on one person's proposal, but he hadn't heard her put forward a better idea.

The words were said as a challenge, and Cressida met it. She sniffed in her brother's direction before turning to the viscount and smiling confidingly.

"I do have a plan, my lord," she said, looking so earnest that Jack smiled in reflex. "A very good plan." She nodded, and Jack's smile grew.

"Well?" the viscount prompted, eager to hear it.

"Would you mind very much, my lord," the angelic Cressida Carrington asked, reaching out to place a hand on his knee as her china blue eyes pleaded with him, and her cherry lips smiled, "breaking your leg?"

Chapter Thirteen

That question quickly wiped the smile from Jack's face, and he stared at Cressida in stunned amazement as Edward hooted, "*That's* your idea, you silly chit? That he should break his *leg?*"

Cressida gazed at them both in some surprise, then nodded. "But of course," she said, looking expectantly at the viscount. "If you had only been good enough to do so the first time, we would not be having this discussion now, for a broken leg takes longer to heal than your sprain, and I'm sure Julia wouldn't think of your leaving until your leg was quite mended, so you wouldn't be leaving now, and Julia would have the time she needs to get used to the idea of your being around and her depending on you—for Julia isn't much used to depending on others, since we are all so used to depending on her. So would you mind very much?"

She was smiling so ingenuously at him that it took several moments for her meaning to penetrate the viscount's befuddled brain, at which point he rose from his chair and, taking a hasty step toward the fireplace, said that he would mind very much. He did not intend to break a leg for anyone, thank you. And he could not help adding that he did not know what kind of a fool Julia Carrington would think him if he did so simply to remain.

"Oh." Cressida's face fell, and she heaved a heavy sigh. "That seems rather disobliging of you, I think."

The viscount was saved from replying by Edward, who gave it as his opinion that his sister was the greatest ninny who ever lived, and he thought his plan much better—the viscount should make a push with Julia and get it over with.

That statement brought instant disagreement from Cressida, and the viscount watched for several moments as brother and sister argued. Since he was much more in favor of Edward's plan than of Cressida's, having turned an idea similar to Edward's over in his mind that afternoon for several hours, the viscount was disappointed when Cressida again voiced the conclusion he had reached staring at the ceiling—it was too soon for Julia to realize the viscount might *wish* to make her responsibilities his own, and the lady might very well turn him away in a manner that would make it nearly impossible for him to approach her again.

"For she is quite determined that you go away, you know," Cressida said, nodding toward the viscount. "She says she feels it is best for the children's sake—they are growing so attached to you, and we all remember how they moped about for weeks after Uncle William left last time. But I think it is for her sake, too."

"You do?" It was one of the few hopeful things Jack had heard that night, and Cressida smiled at his eager tone.

"Oh, yes," she told him. "Although she will never admit it—perhaps not even to herself."

"Oh." The word was a flat monosyllable, and Jack hunched his shoulders forward. "There are any number of women, you know, who do not seem to find the idea of caring for me—repugnant."

It occurred to him that he had made that statement several

times since coming to Carrington Place, and the viscount frowned.

Cressida smiled at him in a manner markedly similar to her older sister's, and said soothingly that she was sure that was true. She added that she did not believe Julia found the idea of caring for him repugnant, either.

"It is just that she places no great confidence in a man's willingness to remain where he is needed, you see," Cressida explained. "After all, Papa went away, and Uncle William, and you are known for—"

"I know," Jack interrupted, running an impatient hand through his hair, "I know! I am known as a thoughtless fribble, a man about town, a care-for-nobody. . . ."

He was waiting for someone to interrupt with a disclaimer; when no one did he frowned at his audience and said that his reputation was greatly exaggerated. Edward looked at him in surprise.

"Then you did not once drive your phaeton ten times through a narrow gate, blindfolded?"

Well, yes, Jack said, he had done that.

"And you do not box regularly with Gentleman Jackson?"

Well, yes, Jack said, he did.

"And you did not once lose twenty thousand pounds at faro, only to win thirty thousand the next night?"

An exasperated Jack said that he did not know where Edward had heard such things, but yes—yes, he had done that. In his younger days.

"I thought it was last year," said the ever-helpful Edward, who asked if it was true Jack had once had two ladybirds in keeping at the same time.

"*What?*" The viscount, his cheeks flushed, stared at the young man in dismay and cast a quick glance toward Cressida, who was regarding them in puzzlement.

"You keep birds, my lord?" she asked politely.

The viscount coughed and said no, no; he had let them all go. He glared at Edward, who had the grace to blush, and beg Lord Chalmsy's pardon, saying he had rather forgotten Cressida was there. . . .

Noting the puzzlement in his sister's eyes, Edward said briskly that yes, well, it was no matter, and not getting them anywhere with their plan to allow the viscount to remain at Carrington Place a bit longer to woo Julia.

"I don't know why you'd want me to wed your sister if you've heard all those things about me and believed them," Jack said, frowning at Edward. The young man shrugged.

"We like you," he said simply. "And we know if you were married to Julia you'd be too busy for such things. She'd see to it."

"We think you have a good heart," Cressida added, when it appeared her brother's words had done little to appease the viscount. Then she paused.

Jack saw her head tilt to the side and waited for the thought to follow. He did not have to wait long. "A black temper, but a good heart. Julia says all you need is a little managing to rid you of the first, and bring out the latter."

"Oh, she does, does she?" The viscount was pleased to hear Julia talked about him, but he was not nearly as pleased with what she had to say. "That's something a managing woman *would* say, I believe!"

Cressida nodded. "So we have to devise a plan to allow you to stay and grow on Julia."

"Give you more of a chance to insinuate your way into her heart," Edward seconded.

Jack, who felt their conversation made him sound like a mold or a sneak, frowned slightly, then shrugged. "I will not break a leg," he told them, ignoring the disappointment on

Cressida's face. "But perhaps we can think of something else."

They sat up long into the night, and they thought of many things. Unhappily, nearly all of them involved some physical—and catastrophic—injury to the viscount, or some act that Lord Chalmsy said he would not perform, even for Miss Carrington, because he did not see how making a complete cake of himself would further his cause with the lady.

When they at last parted for the night they had come up with no better plan than that Jack should ride out from London from time to time to see them, but that, Cressida said pessimistically, was not much good, for like as not Julia would be gone when he arrived, or worse yet, the vicar would make a push for her, and who knew what would happen then?

Jack, whose dislike of the vicar by this time surpassed that of all the younger Carringtons combined, said, "You don't really think Julia would have him, do you?" in tones of such utter loathing that Cressida and Edward took him even closer to their hearts. Unfortunately, they could not say with certainty that such an event was totally beyond the realm of possibility.

"I told you," Edward said glumly. "The man looks at her as if she's the last cake, and he's going to have her."

"Well, he's not!" Jack said, pounding his cane for emphasis. It was unfortunate that his aim was slightly off and he hit his foot instead of the floor, which caused him to yowl and come quickly to his feet, to take several hobbling steps. "Not if I have to knock his lights out and carry Julia off across my saddle, to save her!"

Cressida said kindly that it was a heroic picture, but she rather thought Julia would not appreciate being tossed across the viscount's saddle. Edward added that it would be best not to get his sister's back up, if Lord Chalmsy wanted to find his way into her good graces.

In spite of himself Jack grinned at their practicality, then bade them good night, suggesting that they each see if a brilliant plan wouldn't come to them in their dreams.

Alas, when the comfortable carriage bearing the earl of Clangstone's coat of arms drew up outside Carrington Place the next day, no brilliant plan had yet presented itself, and it was four glum younger Carringtons who watched the coach's approach from the morning room windows. William ran through the french doors at the end of the room to tell the viscount, who sat on the veranda with Julia, looking out at the day, that his brother had arrived (for Jack had told them he expected it would be Charles who came for him), and in a bang-up carriage pulled by prime blood, too!

"Well, then," Julia said, putting down the mending she'd been working on as they sat talking so that she could rise to greet their visitor. "I suppose that's that."

Miss Carrington was smiling, and Jack, watching her closely, thought that perhaps the smile was a shade over bright, but he could not really tell. Miss Carrington had herself well in hand, and was moving through the french doors to make Jack's brother welcome.

Viscount Chalmsy, limping along behind her, had his thoughts interrupted by Lily's announcement that it wasn't the viscount's brother who had come to fetch him—it was a lady!

"A *lady?*" Julia repeated, looking questioningly back toward Jack. He limped forward several more steps to peer out the window.

"Arabella!" the viscount said in astonishment. He

watched as his sister-in-law, after shaking out her skirts and adjusting the cuffs on her jacket, turned back to the carriage and reached inside it for something—a something the viscount saw was her small son as she once more turned toward the house.

"And Baby Jack!"

"A baby!" Lily said, jumping up and down. "Look, Julia, a baby!" The little girl raced from the room and toward the door where the knocker now sounded, getting there before the butler to throw the door open and announce, with a bobbed curtsy, "How do you do? My name is Lily, and may I play with your baby, please? May I?"

Arabella, at once charmed by the child's obvious delight in the joy of Arabella's life, laughed and said, reaching out a hand, "How do you do, Lily? This is Jack, and I am sure he would be delighted to play with you!"

"Lily, my dear."

Arabella turned toward the calm voice that interrupted their conversation and looked critically at the slender brown-haired woman moving gracefully toward her. The woman was dressed in a gown of warm rose that was neat and well made, if not in the first stare of fashion, and she was followed by Jack, a boy a few years older than the child who had greeted her, a pleasant-faced young man, and quite the loveliest young woman Arabella had ever seen.

Oho, Arabella thought, staring at the beauty, whose blond good looks were highlighted by a gown of Cressida's favorite blue. So this is what has occupied Jack's time!

Mrs. Carlesworth gazed speculatively at her brother-in-law, who did not seem at all happy to see her, until her attention was reclaimed by the brown-haired woman whose manner made it clear she was in charge.

"Please, do come in," the woman said. "I am Julia Carrington, and you have met my sister, Lily. May I also present my brother Edward, my sister Cressida, and my brother William." She gestured to each of the others as she spoke, waiting until the named person had made his bow or her curtsy before going on. "May I take your baby for you? I am sure after traveling this distance you would like some refreshment. I will order tea, and Lily, William, and I will entertain young Jack while you refresh yourself."

She held out her hands as she spoke and Arabella, about to demur, was considerably surprised when her son reached out to Miss Carrington. Baby Jack had reached the bashful stage where he wanted no one but his mama, which had accounted for his accompanying her today, her little man having refused loudly and with great, fat tears, to be parted from her as she prepared to leave the house. Yet now he practically leaped from her arms and settled his head comfortably against Miss Carrington's shoulder, one fat little fist going out to clutch the lady's hair.

"You seem to have a way with children, Miss Carrington," Arabella said approvingly. She looked at her brother-in-law and added, a sparkle in her eye, "I imagine that gave you an advantage in dealing with the older Jack."

She was rewarded with a glare from the viscount and a smile from Miss Carrington. It was a lovely smile, Arabella thought, starting at the lady's lips and spreading upward to her expressive eyes.

"We have all enjoyed having Lord Chalmsy with us," Julia said.

"Oh?" Arabella looked so surprised that Julia grinned. Behind her Jack growled, "Cut line, Bella," a comment that seemed to give his sister-in-law considerable satisfaction.

"I do hope he was not completely impossible," Arabella said, ignoring the viscount by fixing her gaze solely upon Miss Carrington.

"Oh, completely," Julia replied, with a mischievous glance upward at Lord Chalmsy, who stood right at her shoulder. "I doubt it is in his nature to be otherwise."

"Now, see here—" Jack protested. He was cut off by his sister-in-law.

"True." Arabella said, shaking her head sadly. "I have remarked on it countless times. It is a great trial to me, I assure you."

"I can imagine," Julia said, her sympathetic nod making it clear she understood.

"I am here," the viscount informed them. "And I would appreciate it if you would not talk about me as if I were not!"

Arabella looked at him in surprise. "But Jack!" she protested. "My love, surely you realize I talk about you *much* worse when you are *not* here!"

The viscount, who saw nothing funny in that statement, was considerably incensed when Miss Carrington burst into laughter—a laughter shared by Lord Chalmsy's exasperating sister-in-law.

"Where is Charles, anyway?" the viscount demanded. "Why didn't *he* come?"

Arabella said that her husband was in York on business; he'd left the day before Miss Carrington's letter arrived and wasn't expected back for another week. The earl had been intent on coming, but his gout was acting up, and Arabella did not want him racketing about the countryside in pain, so she'd decided to come to fetch the viscount home, and to bring the baby, both of them having been confined to the house by Baby Jack's recent illness, and both of them in need of a change of scene and some fresh country air.

"Well, you could have waited for Charles to return," the ungrateful viscount told her, to which she replied that she could not in good conscience inflict Lord Chalmsy upon the Carrington's another week.

"Inflict—" Jack seemed to choke on the word, and an anxious Cressida informed their visitor that it was no such thing. The viscount had been quite the gentleman—

"*Jack?*" Arabella asked, incredulous, and her eyes widened in surprise.

"Cut line, Bella," Jack said again, which caused the lady to laugh. Julia, watching her, liked the laugh, and liked the lady, and wished that she might get to know her better— something she knew would not occur, for Arabella Carlesworth and her brother-in-law would be going back to their London lives that very afternoon, and Julia Carrington would never see them again. . . .

"I'll see about tea," Julia said, clutching the baby to her as she started down the hall, followed by Lily and William. "Cressida, Edward—why don't you take our guests out onto the veranda, and see them comfortably settled. Tea will be ready shortly."

Chapter Fourteen

"Lovely," Arabella said a half hour later as she sat by her brother-in-law looking out over the lawn and garden of Carrington Place. Perhaps thirty feet away Cressida Carrington sat on a blanket holding young Jack on her lap while Lily and William made faces that had the baby laughing with delight.

"Yes, isn't she?" Jack said, but in such an indifferent tone that it gave Arabella pause. If it wasn't leaving the blond beauty that made her brother-in-law look so sulky, then what?

"I, of course, am more drawn to the oldest sister," Arabella said. She watched as Jack's eyes turned toward Julia Carrington, who with Edward had left them to go rescue one of Lily's kittens from a tree into which Sir Lancelot had chased it.

"So much character in that face!" Arabella said, her lips pursed in speculation as her brother-in-law's morose expression grew even more so. "She must be a very strong and intelligent woman to run this house as she does, and to care for her younger brothers and sisters."

"Yes." This time Jack's tone was anything but indifferent. "Strong, and stubborn, and quite possibly the most maddening woman I have ever met, and that is going it some, Bella, for her to be more maddening than you."

His sister-in-law surprised him into silence by clapping her hands together and gurgling in delight. "So that's the way it is! You've fallen in love with the *sensible* sister! How remarkably wise of you Jack—and so out of character! I had quite despaired of you, you know!"

"Thank you," the viscount said, frowning at her, his tone forbidding. "I am sure I know how to take that."

"Oh, yes!" She nodded seraphically at him. "I am sure you do, too!" She giggled again as Jack's frown darkened.

"Yes, well," the viscount muttered, "have a good laugh at my expense, Bella, for you've got your wish. I've fallen in love, just as you wanted. And she's sending me away!"

The pained way in which the last sentence was uttered effectively wiped the smile from Arabella's face, and she looked questioningly toward Jack. He was glaring at the unconscious Miss Carrington as she reached up for the kitten that Edward, who had climbed to the rescue, was handing down to her from his perch in the tree.

"Oh!" Arabella said.

Jack's gaze returned to his sister-in-law, and he eyed her broodingly. "Yes," he agreed. "Oh."

"You want to stay?"

The viscount shrugged. "What I want," he said crossly, "seems to matter to no one! But yes—" He met her eyes, then looked away. "I want to stay."

"Until—?" Arabella prompted.

"Until she realizes I intend to stay forever, of course!" Jack said, more crossly still. "Until she realizes I do love her, and she should love me, too!"

Arabella smiled.

"You know, Jack," his sister-in-law said, rising suddenly, "I think you and I should take a little walk before we return to London. To shake the fidgets out of your legs, you know, before getting into the carriage."

"What?" Jack looked up at her in surprise but rose when she took his hand and tugged commandingly on it. Julia, walking back toward them, the kitten in her hands, looked hesitant as she asked if they must leave so soon.

"Oh, no!" Arabella said, smiling brightly at their hostess, "It is just that I have asked Jack to stroll about your delightful gardens with me for a few minutes, and to take me down to that lovely little pond we can see from here—I am still feeling cramped from the carriage, you know!"

Julia nodded, but slanted a puzzled glance toward the viscount; while the Carrington Place gardens were pleasant enough, Julia thought it a stretch to call them delightful and as for the pond—well, it was really quite ordinary; no fountains to grace it or bright red-gold fish swimming about. Lord Chalmsy gave an ungracious shrug in answer to her unspoken question and offered his arm to his sister-in-law. They strolled off together, but as soon as they were out of Miss Carrington's hearing Jack said, "You know, Bella, I am not in the mood for admiring nature, so—"

The lady pinched his arm warningly as they passed Cressida Carrington with the children, and Arabella said loudly, "You are quite right, Jack—there is a Grecian influence I find most soothing."

Cressida, the baby in her lap, looked up in surprise, then glanced around the gardens with a question in her eyes. If there was a Grecian influence no one had told her; she must, she decided, ask Julia about it.

The viscount, staring down at his sister-in-law in stunned silence, could only nod woodenly. He waited until they were out of earshot to ask her what in the world she thought looked Grecian in the garden.

Arabella gazed limpidly up at him and said that it was the best she could think of on such short notice; besides, wasn't it possible there *was* a Grecian influence somewhere?

"In Greece," Jack said, his voice dry. "And I very much doubt you would recognize it there, either, Arabella!"

His sister-in-law giggled and admitted that was true, then changed the subject with an order to tell her everything that had been going on at Carrington Place since Jack's arrival, and to leave nothing out. At first he refused, but under her determined goading the viscount at last complied, ending his tale with, "And I thought and thought all night, but have come up with nothing to postpone my leaving. Cressida, the silly chit, suggested I break my leg."

He realized Arabella was eyeing him speculatively, and hurriedly added, "But that I won't do, for love or money."

"It would answer," Arabella said, nodding as if it were the most reasonable request ever made. The viscount frowned at her.

"No."

Arabella sighed. "You know, Jack," she said, "the path of true love never did run smooth. Look at Charles and me."

She was pardonably incensed when the viscount said he would rather not, adding with more truth than tactfulness that the lengths to which she had gone to bring his brother to the sticking point were still a source of uneasiness between himself and Charles.

By now they were standing by the small pond; Arabella had removed her gloves and was pulling them thoughtfully from one hand to the other. She fired up at his last remark to say that it was nonsense. "Charles quite understands now

why I asked you to elope with me, and we are so very happy
that he knows it was for the best—it got him to act, you see!"

Seeing the skeptical gleam in her brother-in-law's eye,
she added, "It's true!"

Jack shrugged. "You are quite shameless, Bella," he told
her. "I don't know why I've told you all this, for I'm sure
that any plan you would concoct would be beyond belief."

"Faint heart never won fair maid," Arabella returned.

Jack shook his head at her and turned to start back to the
house. He did not see his sister-in-law lift one of her gloves
and toss it to the obliging wind, which deposited it in the pond.

"Oh!" Arabella cried, distress evident in her voice. "Jack!
My glove! My favorite gloves!"

The viscount turned back in surprise and saw the reason
for her distress as her glove lay floating on the water.

"How—" he started. Arabella did not let him finish.

"Rescue it for me, Jack," she commanded. "My favorite
gloves!"

Reacting to the worry in her voice, the viscount picked up
a stick that lay by the water's edge and leaned forward to
fish the glove from the water. He was shocked when, off-
balance, he felt a hard push from behind and fell face first
into the pond.

"What the—" he exploded, trying to regain his footing.
When he had done so and started out of the pond a determined Arabella gave him a hard push back, so that he
slipped in the mud and sat down suddenly, staring up at her
in astonishment. He was unaware of the lily pad perched
like an epaulet on his shoulder.

"Oh, Jack!" Arabella screamed. "You poor boy! Miss
Carrington, come quick! Jack has reinjured his ankle and
cannot get up. Oh, oh, oh!"

"What—"

The viscount, trying once again to rise, was hissed back into a sitting position by his sister-in-law. She leaned forward and said, the words coming out low and fast, "Don't you dare get up, Jack, for I'm giving you more time here. If you won't be so obliging as to break your leg, you can at least pretend you've hurt your ankle again. It should keep you here for another week—perhaps two, if you nurse it. And if you can't convince Miss Carrington that she loves you and ought to take you on, in spite of all your flaws, in that amount of time, then I wash my hands of you, I do! Now, sit still and moan!"

The viscount, who did, perforce, sit still, refused to moan. He watched in astonishment as his sister-in-law, now surrounded by concerned Carringtons, cast herself into Julia Carrington's arms and sobbed, "It is my fault—all my fault! I dropped my glove and Jack bent to retrieve it for me, and lost his balance, and now he has reinjured his ankle, and his grandfather and my husband will be so vexed with me, and oh, my dear Miss Carrington, I am so sorry, but I am afraid he will not be able to travel today—not for several days, in fact, perhaps several weeks—and I do hate to burden you with him; indeed, I know I should not ask, but—but—"

By this time John also had appeared at the pond, and he and Edward were fishing the viscount out of it. John frowned when he heard Edward whisper, "I knew you'd think of something! Good show!" to the viscount, but said nothing, just looked at his master under his beetling brows. Jack, running a dripping hand through his equally dripping hair, discovered the lily pad upon his shoulder and removed it.

The viscount was as conscious of the smiling faces of the

four younger Carringtons as he was of the bemused expression on their oldest sister's face, and said, his words directed to Julia alone, "I do not wish to trouble you any further—"

Four Carringtons chorused that it was no trouble at all and Arabella, glaring at him from the shelter of Julia's arms, looked very much as if she would like to push him into the pond again.

"Tell him it is no trouble, Julia," Cressida said in her soft voice.

The viscount said that he was sure that, with his foot propped on a pillow, he could travel.

"But no!" Arabella shrugged off Miss Carrington's comforting arms and frowned at him. "You cannot!"

It occurred to her that her vehemence had surprised those around her, and she turned to Julia to say, apologetically, "It is just that my husband and grandfather-in-law, the earl, dote on Jack, you know. And he has always been given to inflammations of the lung, and if he were to take cold riding back to London in that drafty carriage . . . And his ankle, you know; Charles is going to be so angry with me."

Tears welled over Arabella's lower lids and slid down her cheeks. Miss Carrington, in an effort to comfort her charming guest, did not even blink at the characterization of the finest carriage she'd ever seen as "drafty," although she noticed that Jack did. Nor did she remark that when Arabella's husband had visited them earlier he had characterized his brother as "healthy as a horse—hardly ever even has a cold, you know."

Instead she said that of course the viscount must remain at Carrington Place, they would be happy to have him. Although she believed he had been ready to go, and would find it terribly boring, remaining with them . . .

It was a clear question, and Jack, shaking the water out of his eyes and managing a sneeze, at which Arabella nodded approvingly, paused to study Julia's face for a long moment. Then he said, very deliberately, without a hint of a smile, "No, Miss Carrington, I won't be bored. I won't be bored at all."

Lily and William wondered what it was that suddenly turned Julia's cheeks bright red, and made Cressida, Edward, and Arabella smile as Julia stuttered out a, "Well, then! John and Edward can carry you back to your room, and I shall send for the doctor—"

"The doctor!"

Julia stared in amazement at Arabella, Jack, Cressida, and Edward as the shocked words came from their mouths and the four exchanged glances. A disgusted John, looking from the viscount to Arabella and back again, said for Miss Carrington not to worry herself; he'd watched the doctor as he tended the viscount and John was quite sure he could make his master comfortable. At Julia's look of uncertainty he added the diplomatic suggestion that he'd do his best and then, if the viscount wanted, the doctor could be sent for later.

"Splendid idea!" Lord Chalmsy said, patting his groom's shoulder approvingly. John frowned up at him.

"Splendid!" agreed Cressida and Edward.

Julia turned toward Arabella. "But I am sure you would feel better if the doctor examined the viscount—" she began.

Arabella gave an airy wave. "Oh, no!" she said. "John is good with all kinds of animals, you know! I have heard Charles say so time out of mind! I am sure he will take very good care of Jack!"

"Well, then . . ." Julia hesitated.

Lord Chalmsy, feeling it best not to continue the discussion, gave a hearty, "That's settled, then," and allowed himself to be half carried, half dragged toward the house as the ladies trailed behind, Arabella chattering all the way about what a terrible inconvenience it was for the Carringtons to be burdened with Jack for an even longer time, and how she knew he was not an easy guest, so arrogant, and bossy, and demanding as he was, until the viscount itched to box her ears.

John, deriving a certain satisfaction from his master's evident disgust, grunted agreement to each of Arabella's statements, adding under his breath that there'd just better be a groom in Lord Chalmsy's employ who'd be seeing a bit of extra in his wages from then on, for the shifts he was put to were more than an honest man should have to stand.

The viscount, after one indignant glare, shrugged and muttered, "Oh, very well." Edward, privy to the conversation, saw John smile, and then the viscount, and grinned in spite of himself. Life had certainly grown more interesting since Lord Chalmsy arrived at Carrington Place!

Chapter
Fifteen

"I suppose," Arabella said, closely watching Julia Carrington's face over a restoring cup of tea, "that this is a great disappointment, having Jack foisted upon you for another week or two. I can quite understand your eagerness to have him go. I know how impossible he can be—better than anyone, I imagine, for we—"

She had started to say "are so much alike," then thought better of it. It occurred to Arabella that until things were settled between Miss Carrington and Jack, it might be best if the lady seated across from her did not know of the close resemblance Arabella recognized between herself and her brother-in-law.

"We—" Julia prompted politely, eliciting a dainty shrug from her guest.

"—are always rubbing against each other so," Arabella substituted, with a smile. "And as I was saying, my dear, you have my absolute sympathy."

"Oh, no!" Julia put her cup down and rose, taking a hasty step around the room before returning to stand before Arabella, her face earnest. "You must not think we wished the viscount to leave—far from it! He has been so kind to the children; they quite dote on him, really. But we are so removed from his world—from *your* world—living quietly as we do, and of course I perfectly understand why he cannot wait to return to London."

"Oh?" Arabella raised a polite eyebrow, and sipped her tea. "I believe Jack told me it was you who could not wait for him to return to London."

Julia sank back onto the couch and looked toward the window before replying, her words so quiet Arabella had to strain to hear them. "He must think what he wishes, of course."

Arabella smiled inwardly, then arranged a look of polite inquiry on her face as she said, "Is it possible, then, Miss Carrington, that you really will not mind Jack remaining in your home until he is quite well?"

"Of course we will not mind!" Julia realized the force with which the words had been uttered and returned her gaze to her guest. She offered up a weak smile as she continued. "As I said, the children—"

"But you, Miss Carrington," Arabella interrupted. "You have said Jack is very good with the children. It does not surprise me—Jack is such a child himself! But you." Arabella gave her a sympathetic look. "I imagine he has been a real bear, hasn't he?"

"Oh, yes!" Julia smiled in memory and Arabella, watching carefully, detected fondness in the smile. "He is not at all used to having his will crossed, you know!"

"I do know!" Arabella agreed with great feeling. "Yes, I *do* know! And he is an overbearing, arrogant, quick-tempered lout, given to shouting first and thinking later. He cannot stand to be denied, and he is so contrary that if you tell him the sky is blue today, he will immediately call it green, and nothing you say can move him!" She noticed with satisfaction that Miss Carrington was smiling, as if at another memory, and took a quick sip of tea before adding quietly, "I cannot imagine why we love him so."

"No . . ." Miss Carrington agreed abstractly, then started, her cheeks flaming red as she quickly added, "You are his family, of course. So it is only natural that you love him. You, and his grandfather and brother—"

Julia realized she was stuttering and stopped midsentence, further flustered by the wide-eyed look the viscount's sister-in-law directed toward her.

"I am sure that is what you meant," Julia said firmly.

"But of course!" Arabella maintained her gravity with difficulty and kept her eyes wide, for effect. "Whatever else could I have meant?"

Then, taking pity on Miss Carrington, who Arabella was coming to like more every moment, she put her teacup down and rose. With a smile Arabella said she would just look in on Jack before she and her son returned to London to tell the earl about his grandson's latest misfortune.

At mention of the earl Julia looked worried, and asked again if Arabella wouldn't rather they called the doctor in to see to the viscount's latest injury. "I know Dr. Smythley can be annoying," Julia said, "but not for the world would I have your grandfather or husband—or you!—think we have overlooked any effort to care for Lord Chalmsy. I would be happy to send Edward to fetch the doctor—"

"Oh, no!" Arabella said, so hastily that Miss Carrington looked at her in surprise.

"That is," Arabella continued with her best smile, "Jack will actually do much better with John to look after him. They've been together for years, you know, and John is quite devoted to my brother-in-law. He doesn't fret Jack as the doctor would. I know my husband and the earl will feel Jack is in good hands while John is with him."

"Yes, but—"

Arabella thought it sweet that Miss Carrington was so clearly worried about Lord Chalmsy, and said so. Julia blushed.

"Please," Miss Carrington said, the word coming out almost as if she were suffocating. "You must not think—"

Julia held one hand out as if in supplication, and Arabella surprised her by taking the hand and squeezing it warmly.

"I think my disreputable brother-in-law is very lucky to have fallen into your kind and capable hands, Julia Carrington," Arabella said kindly, "and I am very happy to make your acquaintance. And I'll tell you what," she added, when it seemed Miss Carrington was about to interrupt, "I will speak with John, and if he feels there is any reason—any reason at all—to send for the doctor, I shall ask him to speak to you, so that you might do so immediately. There, does that make you feel better?"

It was so evident that Arabella believed her plan satisfactory that Julia felt she could do no more than nod. After all, if the viscount's sister-in-law said the doctor would only fret Lord Chalmsy, and John could handle him much better, who was Julia Carrington to argue?

Jack had changed out of his wet clothes into dry ones when Arabella tripped into his room after the briefest of knocks. John was just finishing wrapping his ankle, ignoring Lord Chalmsy's arguments that there was no reason for that, because they both knew his ankle wasn't injured at all, and he didn't want his foot wrapped up so deucedly tight, so he'd have to hobble around—

"Oh, no!" Arabella said when she heard the last of his mutterings, "No hobbling, Jack! You've reinjured your ankle, remember, and you're to stay in that bed for at least a week. And of *course* your ankle must be wrapped—Miss Carrington is not stupid, you know, and she will realize you're trying to trick her if you're not tied to your bed with your foot propped on an appropriate pillow. You might moan now and then in her presence, too, you know—for sympathy. It strikes me that Miss Carrington is a most sympathetic woman, and would pity anyone who moaned in pain."

"I don't *want* her pity!" Jack shouted, then glared at his groom and sister-in-law as both immediately hushed him. Arabella, inspecting John's work, told the groom it was quite good. John beamed at the praise, and was more than willing to follow her suggestion that he take himself off for a few moments so she could enjoy a comfortable coze with the viscount.

Jack, continuing to glare, begged the groom not to leave. "She'll probably kill me next time she gets me alone," he said.

The viscount was incensed when Arabella giggled and John offered up one of his rare grins before quitting the room.

"Well, Jack," Arabella said when they were alone, "I think we did that rather neatly, don't you?"

The viscount's glare doubled. "Neatly?" he repeated. "Making me an object of pity and tying me to this bed? I think not! How am I supposed to properly court the woman when you've told her I can't walk?"

Arabella opened her eyes very wide at him. "Why, Jack," she said, "I was under the impression that if anyone knew how to conduct a successful dalliance in a bedroom, it was you."

"Arabella!"

The lady watched in amusement as her suave brother-in-law turned bright red.

"You say the most outrageous things!" Jack said, frowning at her. "It is a wonder to me that Charles has not yet strangled you! I do not wish to conduct a dalliance with Miss Carrington—that is—well—"

His sister-in-law appeared as if she might burst into giggles at any moment, and the viscount said threateningly, "If you laugh at me, Arabella, I swear, I shall box your ears! I don't know why Charles doesn't lock you in the attic and leave you there! In fact, I think I shall advise it, the next time I see him!"

Arabella laughed.

"Bella!"

The threatening tone made her laugh louder, but her humor came to an abrupt end when the viscount, switching tactics, said with great interest, "And just what are you going to *tell* my good brother when he returns from York and I'm not in London?"

"Why—" The lady grew quite interested in smoothing a wrinkle from her skirt, "I shall tell him you had another accident, of course—"

"Ha!"

Arabella looked up, and her chin came out. "I suppose *you* are going to tell him I pushed you into the pond!"

"I am."

"And I suppose you'll tell him I have been meddling—"

"I shall most assuredly tell him that!"

The lady bit her lip. "It is very bad of you, Jack, when I am only trying to help you!"

"*Help* me?" In spite of himself, the viscount yelped the words. "*Help* me? By practically *drowning* me, Arabella? By making me out to be a perfect cake, a clumsy oaf who slips into ponds and turns his ankle? By—by—" He could have gone on, but his irrepressible relative was biting her lip. He eyed her suspiciously. "Well?" he asked.

"Oh, Jack!" the lady said. "If you could have seen yourself—dripping wet, with that lily pad on your shoulder—" She went off into gales of laughter, pausing only to wipe her eyes and to say, in short gasps, "And now here you are—saying you'll tell Charles—when we both know you're much too much of a gentleman to upset him that way."

"I *will* tell him, Bella!" Jack threatened. "I swear!"

His sister-in-law wiped her eyes with a small scrap of linen and lace. "Dear Jack!" she said. "So untruthful!"

The viscount frowned. "You have done some foolish things in your time, Bella—"

"But always with the purest of motives!" the lady protested.

"Ha!"

The viscount would have said more but they were interrupted by a tap at the door. Lord Chalmsy, expecting to see John, uttered an impatient "Come in!" He was surprised when Julia Carrington entered the room carrying Baby Jack.

"He's in one of his moods," Arabella offered when Julia looked questioningly toward her.

"I am not!" the viscount snapped, then glared at both women as they exchanged understanding glances. Arabella, reading in his eyes all he'd have liked to say but was prevented from shouting at her by Miss Carrington's presence, rose and grinned down at him.

"Dear Jack," she said, bending forward to sweetly place a kiss on his cheek and to whisper, "This is an opportunity you've been given, Jack—make the most of it, or I swear, I will break your leg myself!"

Lord Chalmsy's jaw dropped and he looked up at her in surprise as she straightened and favored him with another bright smile before turning to collect her son from Miss Carrington.

"Well, Miss Carrington," Arabella said, grinning at the other woman, "I shall take *my* Baby Jack and leave you with yours."

"*Bella!*" The viscount roared. The lady laughed at him, then offered Miss Carrington a sympathetic smile.

"I believe," Arabella said, ignoring the threats the viscount was hurling at her, "that *my* Baby Jack is much easier to handle!" She paused at the door to once again smile at her brother-in-law. "*My* Baby Jack is also much sweeter tempered," she said, bestowing a fond kiss on her small son's head.

Miss Carrington, hearing the insults still being hurled at the lady beside her as the door closed behind them—a lady remarkably unmoved, even cheerful in the face of all that was being said—could only laugh, and nod in agreement.

Chapter Sixteen

"I quite like your sister-in-law," Miss Carrington said that night as she placed his supper tray across the viscount's lap and lifted the covers on the dishes there to show him several slices of the housekeeper's excellent sirloin, served with warm brown bread, potatoes, and green peas. A warm custard awaited his spoon for dessert.

"She's a terrible woman," the viscount returned promptly, appreciating the picture Miss Carrington presented as she bent over him. She was wearing a gown of her favorite spring green, and the color set off her complexion to perfection. A deeper green ribbon was threaded through her hair, and around her neck was a gold locket Jack knew contained small portraits of her parents. "Managing, bossy, quite beyond the pale. She asked me to elope with her once, you know!"

"She *what?*" Miss Carrington, who had seated herself at the viscount's right to keep him company during his meal, was startled out of her usual calm. Lord Chalmsy nodded in satisfaction.

"She did," he said.

"You are making that up!"

"I am not! She asked me to elope with her, and what's more, I did so!"

"But—but—how—" The viscount was enjoying Miss Carrington's bemusement.

"How did she end up married to my brother Charles?" he prompted, when Julia did not seem able to complete her sentence. Miss Carrington nodded. "I'll tell you," the viscount said, spearing a piece of the well-done sirloin with relish. "And then you'll see her for what she is, the little baggage! My sister-in-law is a minx, there's no denying it—and that's putting it politely, too! You'll see!"

What Miss Carrington told him she saw, when his entire story had been told, was that he was very lucky to have a sister-in-law who loved his brother so. The viscount appeared disgruntled.

"I might have known you'd take her side," he grumbled.

Miss Carrington smiled. "And she asked you to run away with her only after you'd assured her you didn't wish to marry her?"

He nodded. "The woman is crazy, you know," he said, finishing off the sirloin and reaching for his custard. "I'm a much better catch than Charles. Everyone knows that!"

"But you weren't a better catch for Arabella," Miss Carrington said. "She obviously knows what she wants, and how to get it."

"Oh, she knows how to get it, all right," the viscount said sarcastically. "By plotting, and scheming, and conniving—"

His glance happened to fall on his ankle, propped comfortably on the pillow Miss Carrington had brought for him, and the viscount stopped abruptly. He felt heat accent his cheeks as he remembered how many times his sister-in-law had told him he and she were just alike. Realizing Miss Carrington was watching him with a question in her eyes, he said, half grudgingly, "Of course, I suppose she'd say her motives are pure. . . ."

Miss Carrington smiled. "One must always take into account pure motives," she replied, rising to remove the tray from his lap. The viscount stared up at her.

"Do you really think so, Miss Carrington?" He delayed her departure by placing his hand on her wrist.

She gazed down at him in surprise, for he sounded so serious. "Why, yes," she said, looking from his face to his hand and back again. "Don't you?"

Jack removed his hand and sighed. "I hope so," he said, staring at his foot again. "I sincerely do."

Miss Carrington, thinking his ankle must be paining him more than she'd first thought, prepared to tactfully withdraw. She promised to return in the morning with breakfast and several books to help him while away the time until his ankle was healed again.

"Books?" Jack said. His face fell as William's did when he was denied his third helping of his favorite sweet.

"Why, yes." Julia smiled down at him. "I would imagine you would like something to do while you are tied to your bed."

Jack sighed. "I was hoping," he said, glancing up at her and then staring pitifully off toward the corner, "that you might help me pass the time."

Miss Carrington was much too knowledgeable in the tactics of young boys bent on getting their own way not to recognize those same tactics in an older male, and she bit her lip to keep back the laughter bubbling up in her throat.

"Oh?" she said.

Jack sighed again, and picked disconsolately at the quilt top. "I suppose, though," he said, still staring at the corner, his mouth turned mournfully down, "that you are too busy to spare me an afternoon—or even a thought. Why would anyone want to sit with me in this bedroom when they could be out in the garden, sitting in the sun, or riding across the fields?"

"Why indeed?" Miss Carrington agreed, causing Jack to look quickly up in surprise, and then away again, as if deeply hurt by her comment.

"Of course," he continued, as if she hadn't spoken, "*I* shall be here. All alone. In this room. By myself."

This time Jack did not need to fake the sigh that escaped his lips, and Miss Carrington took pity on him. Although she recognized the shifts gentlemen of all ages go to to get their own ways, she laughed at herself to realize she was not immune to them. She wondered about that, and decided to consider it later.

"Well," Miss Carrington said. The hesitancy in the word made Jack look hopefully toward her. "If you think you will be lonely . . ."

"I will," Jack assured her, nodding his head up and down with the vigor of a very well man. Miss Carrington puzzled over that as she watched him. "I really will."

"Then I shall tell Lily and William they must visit you daily, and read their catechisms to you," Miss Carrington said, hugely enjoying the look of horror that spread over the viscount's face as she pretended not to see it at all. "We would not want you to be lonely, or to feel neglected in any way."

"But—" Lord Chalmsy sputtered. "But—"

"And Cressida can come and tell you about the kittens, and her flowers," Miss Carrington continued. "I know Edward would be delighted to discuss London with you for hours—I will certainly ask him to do so! I believe he has a thousand questions about London dress and London sights and London manners—"

"*Manners?*" Jack repeated, the word coming out high and strangled.

Miss Carrington nodded. "He will hang on your every word, I am sure."

"But—" It was all Jack could do not to bound from the bed and take several hasty turns around the room in frustration; he had started to rise when he remembered his supposedly injured ankle, and he fell back against the pillows with a vengeance, frowning at Julia in a way that would make her smile each time she remembered it as she readied herself for bed that night.

"I believe," Jack said, his jaw tight, "that I espoused a desire for *your* company, Miss Carrington. If you find that thought distasteful you need only say so; you need not disrupt your brothers' and sisters' lives in that way. I am surprised you can even *consider* asking *them* to take on a task *you* find so abhorrent! I do not, as I believe I have said before, wish to be a *burden* to anyone."

Watching him, Julia could barely contain herself; besides the urge to laugh, she felt her fingers itch to brush back the strand of thick dark hair that had fallen across his forehead as his temper rose.

Instead, she held on to his supper tray and feigned surprise.

"*My* company?" she repeated. "*My* bossy, managing, overbearing, stubborn company?"

A stunned expression replaced the sulkiness on the viscount's face, and he gulped in spite of himself.

"Where," he asked, "did you hear that?"

Miss Carrington raised an eyebrow and Lord Chalmsy sighed.

"Arabella." He more breathed than enunciated the word, and Julia smiled.

"Sometimes," the viscount said, his disgust evident, "I really think I will have to drown that woman. I suppose Charles won't like it, but there are some things a man just has to do, despite the consequences."

This time Julia could not help but giggle. "She told me you describe her so all the time, my lord," she assured him, "and she said you only say such things about people you care for—"

Julia stopped abruptly and the words hung between them. Lord Chalmsy was staring keenly at her and Miss Carrington felt her cheeks grow warm; she wondered why she had not heretofore noticed how hot the room had become.

"Yes, well—" Julia said, meeting the viscount's penetrating gaze and turning hastily away, "I'll just be going then, and will bid you good night—"

She moved quickly to the door, but was stopped by Jack's soft, "Julia."

She turned slightly to inform him she had not given him leave to use her name, and he smiled in the heart-stopping way that had been known to make more than a few London ladies' hearts flutter. "Give me leave," he coaxed.

Julia turned back to the door, informing him over her shoulder that it would not be proper, and she had no intention of doing so.

"Are you always proper, my dear?" he asked.

She informed him—and the door, for it was the door she was staring at, not looking back at the viscount despite his best efforts to make her do so—that she was not his dear, and he was not to call her *that,* either.

The viscount smiled. "You may call me Jack," he suggested. "*And* 'my dear.' I assure you I will not mind at all."

Miss Carrington told the door this was a conversation they should not be having, and it would be best if they ended it and never spoke so again. She reached for the doorknob, and hesitated as Jack uttered a soft, "Miss Carrington."

Julia hesitated for several moments before glancing back, cross with herself for blushing like a schoolroom miss. Jack was grinning at her, but with such tenderness in his eyes. . . .

She looked away and said, quite formally, "Is there something else, my lord?"

Then she waited.

"Miss Carrington," the viscount repeated, his voice caressing the words as no one ever had before—in fact, Julia had never before known it was possible to so caress a formal title. "Please. Look at me. I promise I will not bite you. Truly."

An inelegant snort told him what the lady thought of that promise and Jack grinned. Ever courageous, Julia once again turned. She raised an eyebrow as she had seen him do several times when he was on his high ropes and looking extremely haughty. Since she didn't have the viscount's experience at looking haughty the effect was not the same; Jack guessed she would have been considerably discomposed to know the viscount thought she looked adorable.

"Miss Carrington," Jack said, smiling gently at her with a warmth in his eyes that she was confused to see, "say you will come and give me a hand of cards. We will play whatever you will. Edward tells me you are quite good."

"I was used to play with Father," she said absently, looking at him but not quite seeing him, which bothered Jack extremely. "And Mr. Hartwell often likes to play, when I visit him."

"There, you see," Jack said, smiling even more warmly at her, "you are already used to playing cards with invalids. Surely it will not be too much for you to take a hand with me!"

Miss Carrington shook her head at him and said it was no wonder he had earned such a reputation, for he said the most ridiculous things. Invalid, indeed! And he mustn't refer to Mr. Hartwell as one, either, for if that old gentleman ever heard of it, he would appear on the viscount's doorstep demanding satisfaction.

"I tremble at the thought," Lord Chalmsy said, earning himself another smile.

"Yes." Miss Carrington nodded in mock agreement. "I can see you are terrified, my lord."

"Terrified you will not return, Miss Carrington," the gentleman agreed promptly. "And I shall be left here without hope of stimulating conversation. In which case I shall probably go into a decline, and you will be left to explain to my grandfather and brother—and to Arabella, for that matter, although she would probably thank you—just what happened. You do not want my decline on your conscience, do you, Miss Carrington?"

He had assumed a look of such anxious inquiry that Julia could do nothing but laugh, and shake her head at him. A moment later she whisked herself from the room, but not before the viscount had received his promise.

Each afternoon while he was with them she would devote an hour of her time to a game of cards. And, she told him, when it was clear he doubted her skills in comparison with his, she would very likely win.

Chapter
Seventeen

True to her word, Miss Carrington joined his lordship each afternoon for the express purpose of beating him at cards—and, to his obvious enjoyment, she was not overly conscious of keeping their play to an hour.

They were hardly ever alone, for Lily and William, and often Cressida and Edward, came to watch the game. Miss Carrington's younger sisters were highly partisan as they cheered her on, and William and Edward took an avid interest in his lordship's play, and were staunchly partisan on his behalf.

At first the viscount, who had hoped afternoons alone with Miss Carrington might provide opportunities for some serious courtship, was disgruntled, but he soon came to realize that a Julia Carrington surrounded by her family was a much more relaxed and open Julia Carrington. The few times they had been alone and he had tried to flatter the lady she had withdrawn from him, offering only monosyllabic responses to his attempts to further their acquaintance.

Then, too—and this also was much to his surprise—Jack soon realized that he *liked* being surrounded by the members of the Carrington family; he enjoyed the easy way they

166

traded support and insults. It occurred to him that he had been alone too long, and he thought with regret of all the times his grandfather and Charles had encouraged him to join them at High Point, where they spent most of the year, and he had refused.

His mornings at Carrington Place were often spent in the company of Lily and William, for the two took it upon themselves to help him pass the hours between breakfast and lunch by moving their schoolroom into his bedroom, and naming him head schoolmaster. Wasn't it lucky, Lily asked him, her young face serious, that their most recent governess had just left them, before he arrived, and Julia had not yet had the opportunity to engage another one?

The viscount, who could think of several epithets besides lucky, was not immune to that wide-eyed gaze, and so resigned himself to hearing lessons and answering the questions that occupied the younger Carrington's minds. He had expected to be bored beyond belief, and was surprised to find that the children had any number of questions he had not before considered in quite their way. If he did not exactly look forward to a morning of sums and reading and questions about Egypt, Italy, and America, he always was reasonably cheerful when the morning was done.

Whether that was because of the children's influence, or because Julia Carrington, when her duties allowed, joined the morning lessons, sitting quietly by the window mending what to Lord Chalmsy's critical eye appeared to be a never-diminishing pile of linen, was not known. The lady listened intently, a soft smile creasing her face whenever one of the children asked an especially astute question.

Although he found being tied to his bed by his supposed injury confoundedly tedious and inconvenient, and more

than once had had to make a diving leap for his bed as
someone approached—for he was given to walking about
the room whenever he was alone—the viscount was recon-
ciled to his enforced inactivity by the hope that Miss Carrington was growing fonder of him. It was a hope shared
and encouraged by Edward and Cressida, who told him together and separately that they believed Julia was becoming quite used to him, and even looked forward to their
afternoons together. Cressida swore there was an added
bloom in her sister's cheeks, and Edward, who couldn't
agree to that, did think there might be a bit more of a twinkle in her eye.

Lord Chalmsy, closely surveying the lady in question the
next time they met, could detect neither a bloom nor a twinkle, but he was encouraged by the way Julia smiled at him,
and asked if he would prefer peas or carrots with his roast
lamb. He was also encouraged when, after Lily and William
had left him Friday morning, she paused as she followed
them out the door with her sewing basket to ask, with the
slightest hesitation, if he felt the children were progressing
as well as they might.

Since Jack thought they were two of the brightest children
he had ever met—and since he didn't bother to mention that
he had met few, children coming little in the way of a man
about town of his age—he was able to assure her that he
thought the children were doing prodigiously well. Miss
Carrington looked relieved and Jack took comfort in the fact
that she had sought his opinion.

He was so pleased that she had done so that he mentioned
it to the next person who entered his room, which happened
to be his faithful henchman, John. Delighted that Julia
seemed to be depending on him even a little bit, he had for

the moment forgotten that John was the one member of the household who knew of his duplicity and heartily disapproved of it. The viscount's euphoria was dashed when the groom, after allowing that the children were smart ones, all right, ended with, "But what is Miss Carrington going to think when she realizes you've been deceiving her all along? Do you think she's going to think she can depend on you then?"

"Oh, John, for goodness' sake!" the viscount said, shrugging impatiently and frowning at his long-time friend. "That face of yours would turn sweet milk sour! There's no reason she really has to know, is there? I'll just recover one of these days! And it's not so very bad, after all; I'm not out to hurt the woman—I want to marry her!"

John muttered something about marriages that begin with lies never prospering, and then added, for good measure, "And don't you think the lady's going to grow suspicious pretty soon, when the first time you hurt yourself you could barely wait to get up and about, and now here you are, lying about in your bed for days, with your foot propped up and you as content as content can be not to move?"

It was probably the fact that what John said echoed the viscount's own unquiet thoughts, but Jack was not about to admit that; instead he frowned and said that as far as that goes, he had already told Miss Carrington that he would try tomorrow to use the cane she'd loaned him, and even hoped he might be able to make the journey downstairs and join her on the veranda.

"Hmmmph," said John, unimpressed. A knock at the door prohibited his saying more, to the viscount's relief, and after casting his employer a look filled with meaning, the groom moved to the door and held it for Cressida Carrington, who came in bearing his lordship's lunch on a tray.

"Here you are," Cressida said, smiling down at him, "and Julia says to tell you she is most sorry, but she won't be able to play cards with you this afternoon; she and Edward must ride over to visit Mr. Hartwell. In fact, they've already gone—some matter about the sheep, I believe. The children and I are going to walk into the village, and Julia suggested that I see if there might be any errand I could execute for you there?"

The viscount, whose face had fallen when told he would be deprived of Miss Carrington's company for the afternoon, frowned a moment and then said no, he could think of nothing—and when would Julia be back?

Cressida's smile grew. "She will join you for supper, sir—in fact, we will all join you, for Julia said we might have a picnic in your room! And then we are going to play jackstraws, and tell ghost stories—that is William's idea—"

"I can hardly wait," Lord Chalmsy said, his tone dry. He tried for a moment to picture the astonishment of his London friends should they hear of his evening's entertainment and, even with his powerful imagination, could not. A rueful smile touched his lips at the thought.

"Is something wrong, Lord Chalmsy?" Cressida's voice was uncertain as she looked down at him. The viscount, giving himself a shake, said no, he rather thought he had a touch of a headache, but otherwise nothing was wrong.

A relieved Cressida said that he could just take a nap that afternoon to rid himself of the ache in his head, since he would have the house to himself. The servants would be there, of course, so if he should have any need—

The viscount shook his head at her and smiled. He assured her John would take good care of him, which made the groom roll his eyes and grunt. Cressida smiled upon them both and departed after adjuring Lord Chalmsy to eat his dinner before it grew cold.

Lord Chalmsy did, but he found the edge was taken off his appetite by the knowledge that he would be spending the afternoon alone. The hours seemed to stretch unendingly before him and he offered John a game of cards, only to be disappointed when the groom declined. John, the viscount learned, planned to take Lord Chalmsy's team for a drive to stretch their legs.

"I'll go with you!" the viscount said, throwing the covers back and starting to stand. The groom frowned at him.

"Oh, very good, sir," John said. "And should any of the servants happen to see you—or should we encounter Miss and Mr. Carrington or that vicar who's always nosing about, or any of the neighbors, by chance, on our drive—what excuse would you be wanting me to give them for your sudden recovery? A miracle, perhaps?"

"I don't know the neighbors," Lord Chalmsy replied, frowning both at the groom's mention of the vicar and at the turn in this conversation. It was not going where he wanted it to.

"Yes, well, you can bet they know you—or of you," John said roundly, his brows beetling as he frowned at his master. "And you know how it is in the country—it would get back to Miss Carrington faster than the cat can sniff cream! And then you'd be in the basket, no mistake!"

"Oh, very well," the viscount said, as ungraciously as he could. His eyes were dark, and his face wore a frown. "I see your point."

Then he brightened. "But perhaps if I went in disguise—"
He looked at John hopefully. "You know, John, you and I
could change clothes and I could take the team out as you,
if I kept your cap pulled far forward and didn't look anyone in the eye. And you could stay here in this room as
me."

John stared at him openmouthed and gave it as his opinion that his lordship hadn't injured his ankle, he'd lost his
mind. Lord Chalmsy, with his broad shoulders and no excess fat on his well-built frame, stood a head and a half taller
than his balding, stockily built groom, and not even in the
dark could one pass for the other, John was sure.

"No, my lord," John said. "No, and no, and no."

In the end a disgusted viscount had to admit his groom
was right, and he stared wistfully toward the window as he
said, his voice dripping with dissatisfaction, "It looks like a
perfect day, too."

"Oh, yes," the groom agreed, and grinned to tease his
master so. "It *is* a perfect day. Blue sky, sunshine, and the
gentlest breeze. Makes a man happy to be alive."

The viscount frowned at him. "You're enjoying this,
aren't you?" he demanded.

John's grin grew. "I'll be sure to tell you all about it when
I return," he promised.

The viscount said that was not necessary.

"But I *want* to," the groom assured him.

"Sometimes," Jack said, frowning even more heavily at
the man, "I don't know why I put up with you."

John chortled. "Because," he replied, his blue eyes twin-
kling under their bushy brows, "I'm the only servant you've
ever had who was willing year in and year out to put up with
you!"

The truth of that statement did not in anyway prevent the viscount from heaving a pillow at his groom as that good man departed the room. Nor was Jack's mood in any way lightened when he heard John laughing all the way down the stairs after the viscount missed.

Chapter
Eighteen

It seemed a much longer afternoon than usual for Lord Chalmsy, who spent a good part of it looking out the window, watching for Miss Carrington to come home, and pacing. Unfortunately the room, while among the more spacious bedchambers in the house, did not provide all the pacing space he would like.

Impatient to be striding across the gardens or mounted upon a horse, the viscount found himself with almost more energy than he could contain. By three o'clock he thought he would burst if he did not do something to alleviate the excess energy within him, and in desperation he dropped to the floor for a round of pushups. He had raised and lowered himself a number of times, and was nose down, about to push up again, when there was a soft rap on the door. That was followed immediately by the sound of the door opening, and a gasped, "My lord!"

The viscount, cursing himself for seven kinds of a fool, recognized the housekeeper's voice and turned his head slightly, so he could see her. The smile he was pinning on his face froze, then disappeared as he saw she was not alone. Standing beside her, his mouth agape, was the vicar.

"Lord Chalmsy!" the good woman said, rushing forward to kneel by his side. "Whatever has happened?"

Seeing the honest distress in Mrs. Weston's face, Jack mustered a smile and rolled to his side, saying sheepishly, with a look known to melt many a lady's heart, "You have caught me, I'm afraid!"

"Caught?" The housekeeper regarded him uncertainly, one hand on his shoulder as she knelt beside him.

"Yes." The viscount nodded, and his sheepish grin grew. "I was trying to walk, and you can see what happened! It was most foolish of me and now here I lie, heartily embarrassed. Please don't tell Miss Carrington. I haven't suffered a hurt to anything but my pride, and I would not for the world worry or distress her."

"No, no!" Mrs. Weston agreed, not proof against the young man's smile or the sincerity in his voice. "Of course not! But you shouldn't have been trying to walk, you know! Not hurt as you are! What you need is a spot of tea. As soon as we get you back into bed, of course . . ."

She started to rise, then stopped, looking down at the viscount in the most distracted way. After a moment she dropped to her knees again. "First we must get you safely tucked up, my lord, and resting comfortably on your pillows! I'll just fetch your man. Oh dear! I do believe he took your team for exercise! Well, don't you worry, I'll fetch help, and we'll have you back in bed in no time!"

Once again she started to rise, then stopped, and put a hand on the viscount's forehead. "You are sure you're all right?" she asked, worry evident in her gaze. "For it's that sorry I am one of us wasn't here to help you."

Jack, suffering a temporary pang at her obvious concern, immediately countered with a soothing, "There is no reason in the world why you should have been with me. And if I weren't such a nodcock, I wouldn't have taken such a tumble! Please—do not worry yourself any further. I am quite all right, and need only a hand up to put me back where I should be. I'll be right as a trivet in no time!"

This time Mrs. Weston did rise. She was hurrying to the door to call for help when the vicar, who had stood unmoving during the previous exchange, stopped her by saying, in his most supercilious tones, "There is no need to call anyone, Mrs. Weston. I am sure I can help his lordship back into bed without bothering the servants. And perhaps if you would bring up that pot of tea you mentioned—?"

It was a clear dismissal, uttered in a tone Jack could only consider high-handed. From the way Mrs. Weston drew herself up he realized she felt the same way; her indignation was even more apparent in the way she looked pointedly at the viscount to ask if he would like to accept the vicar's offer, or if he would prefer she fetch other help.

It occurred to Jack that the housekeeper quite hoped he would cite a preference for the servants, but there was something in the vicar's face that made Lord Chalmsy, always a gambler, decide to play whatever game the man had in mind. The viscount said, in the blandest voice possible, that he would be quite happy to accept the vicar's help—if the vicar thought he could lift him.

That shaft went home.

The vicar, almost as tall as Lord Chalmsy, but without the viscount's breadth of shoulders, was used to hearing himself described as a handsome and well-built man. In truth, if the vicar were one to get puffed up about such things—which, of course, he often told himself he was not, humility being a virtue—the vicar actually did consider himself one of the strongest and most athletic men in the neighborhood.

It was apparent Mrs. Weston also knew an insult among

the upper classes when she heard one, for her face grew much more cheerful. She grinned at the viscount as she bobbed a curtsy before withdrawing with the information that she would be back shortly with the tea, and some of those little cakes he liked.

"I like your cakes, too, Mrs. Weston," the vicar interjected, to which the housekeeper replied with a much less enthusiastic curtsy, and a "To be sure, you do!" which the gentlemen were left to interpret any way they liked.

Jack, with Edward's condemnation of the vicar's appetite ringing in his ears, took her words as a verbal slap, and grinned over them. The vicar seemed to hear nothing amiss, however, and Lord Chalmsy, watching him critically as the man approached, decided that it must be because the vicar had such a high opinion of himself that whenever anyone uttered such a statement, he took it as a compliment, and did not suspect that there might be a hidden—and scornful—meaning behind it.

Jack had a great deal of time to watch the man as the vicar moved ponderously forward. First the visitor walked to the chair by the window to lay down his hat and cane, then he moved slowly back, pausing almost unconsciously at the mirror to check the arrangement of his hair and cravat. It was apparent he detected a slight problem with the latter, for he touched it lightly in several places before giving himself a nod of approval and turning his attention to Jack.

He did not wish to, but the viscount had to admit that the vicar had the sort of florid good looks some women liked—although Jack was convinced Julia Carrington was not and *could not* be among them. It would not surprise Jack if in a few years the vicar's stomach went to paunch, and he thought he detected a little thinning in the hair on the top of the man's head, although that hair was so artfully arranged and pomaded that the viscount could not be sure. The man's smile was unctuous, Jack decided, and all in the all his lordship believed he detested the vicar three times as much as all the children combined.

On that charitable note, he raised himself into a sitting position and waited.

For anyone else Jack would have been as helpful as possible as the person tried to lift him; for the vicar, the viscount very much feared, he would prove dead weight.

"Lord Chalmsy," the vicar said, bowing formally.

Jack managed quite a creditable bow in return, considering his position.

"You have, perhaps, thought it remiss of me not to visit you more often," the vicar began formally, standing over him.

"No," Jack said.

The vicar checked, surprised, then continued with a thin-lipped smile.

"As vicar it is, of course, my duty to visit the sick," the man said, as if instructing Jack in a vicar's duties as he ignored the viscount's response. "I *certainly* would have visited you more often, had I known you were going to be in our neighborhood for such a long time. Of course, I thought—we all thought—you would be gone long before now. When I first heard of your indisposition I assumed it was not serious, and would mend in perhaps two days of quiet." The vicar was frowning down at the viscount, and as his frown grew, Jack's brow lightened.

"We?" Jack said, smiling pleasantly.

The vicar nodded. "Dr. Smythley. Everyone in the neighborhood. Miss Carrington, of course! She told me you were healing quickly, so there was no need for me to take time from my busy schedule and trouble myself with more than that one short visit when we met, and of course I thought one of your reputation would not expect a man of the cloth to—"

The vicar seemed to realize that thought might be construed as impolite, for he said, color rising slightly to his cheeks, "Not, of course, that I am ever too busy to do my duty, and I quite understand that a man of your reputation could benefit greatly from numerous visits from a man of the cloth. Although Miss Carrington was quite insistent that I should not bother myself—"

If Jack had not already fallen in love with Julia Carrington he would have done so then, simply because she had done her best to spare him visits from the vicar.

"My reputation?" Jack said aloud, raising his eyebrow. It was a potent tool, the viscount's eyebrow, and better men than the vicar had been discomfited by it. Under Lord Chalmsy's practiced pretention-depressing gaze, the vicar colored further.

"I have heard," the man said repressively, "stories."

"Oh?" Jack seemed to consider. "I suppose there will always be . . . stories . . . vicar. I even have heard . . . stories . . . about you."

Jack waited a moment to be sure that had gone home, then continued smoothly, "I did not listen to such gossip, of course, for I find gossip a dead bore. I am surprised to hear one of your high moral character and standing does not feel the same."

The vicar, whose lips had compressed during Jack's speech, said stiffly, his back erect, "I cannot believe you, sir, for there are no stories to tell of me, and even if there were, you have been confined to this room, so who you would hear them from, when you see only the Carrington family—"

The ironic gleam in Jack's eye, coupled with another quirk of the viscount's eyebrow, made the other man stop suddenly.

"Miss Carrington would not—" the vicar began.

"I did not say she did," Jack countered smoothly. Hiding an inward grin, the viscount further discomposed his adversary by adding, in his blandest voice, "And as delightful as it is sitting here chatting with you, I think it would be even more delightful from the bed, not the floor."

The vicar, his brows drawn together, snapped "Of course" in a tight voice that showed how deeply the viscount had offended him. Before Jack knew quite what the other man was about, the vicar had reached down from behind the viscount and hauled him up, holding Jack under the arms as he maneuvered him toward the bed, two feet away. Jack found himself pushed face forward down onto the coverlet; he started to turn over just as the vicar raised the viscount's wrapped foot and dropped it onto the bed, catching the heel on the bedpost.

Jack groaned affectingly as Mrs. Weston came through the door with the tea tray. That good woman, aghast, said, "Reverend Stonehall, whatever are you doing?" .

"I was just trying to help Lord Chalmsy with his injured foot—" the vicar started, read the disbelief in both pairs of eyes, and stopped when Jack murmured, "How Christian of you."

That *did* bring the color flooding into the vicar's cheeks, and his jaw tightened but he said nothing more than a terse thank-you to Mrs. Weston as she handed him a cup of tea after tsking several times at him for his rough handling of their guest.

"It's quite all right, Mrs. Weston," Jack soothed her, enjoying the other man's discomfiture. "I'm sure the vicar did not *mean* to be either callous or clumsy, despite what his actions might indicate."

The viscount sipped his tea and smiled inwardly; if the vicar wasn't careful, Jack thought, the man would bite right through that teacup.

Lord Chalmsy picked up one of the cakes Mrs. Weston had placed conspicuously close to his right hand, out of the vicar's reach, and bit appreciatively into it as he waited. He did not have to wait long.

As soon as Mrs. Weston left the room the vicar cleared his throat and, in his best Sunday voice, said, "Lord Chalmsy, I believe we find ourselves in a delicate situation."

Jack, about to take another bite of the cake, stopped with the morsel two inches from his mouth and looked inquiringly toward his visitor. "We do?"

The vicar nodded. It was a slow and heavy nod, weighted with censure. "Miss Carrington," the vicar said, "is unmarried. And in this house alone with you—you, with your reputation. Unchaperoned—"

It was apparent the man was prepared to go on, but Jack's shout of laughter stopped him. The vicar glared at the viscount with patent disapproval. "You find that funny, my lord?" the vicar said, his tone austere.

Jack grinned. "Indeed I do! My dear fellow, Miss Carrington has four younger brothers and sisters, devoted servants, and my dragon of a groom to champion her! I doubt anyone has ever been *less* alone or unchaperoned in a house in their life!"

Stonehall permitted himself a small smile. "Yes," he said, his chin dipping up and down in a slow nod. "I do know of what you speak. I, too, am very aware of the number of Miss Carrington's charges, for they are always popping up just when I most wish to—well."

He stopped and cleared his throat in a way that made Jack's fingers itch to tighten around that part of the gentleman's anatomy. "And I know Miss Carrington is of far too superior a character to succumb to your blandishments, even if you were attracted to good and decent women, which I am sure you are not, for they say the ladybirds you've had in your keeping—well!"

Aware of the imprudence of that train of thought and of the dangerous look in Lord Chalmsy's eye, the vicar cleared his throat again.

"I am sure," the vicar said, at his most sepulchral, "that you understand I say these things to you only because of a strong sense of duty. It is not that I wish to insult you, but sometimes, when Miss Carrington talks of you, I think I see in her eyes—well!"

He stopped again suddenly, much too suddenly for the viscount, who very much wished to know what it was the man saw in Miss Carrington's eyes. "I don't suppose that really matters, because it is probably Miss Cressida Carrington who is most in danger from you, and I am sure her older sister watches her closely, for one can always depend on Miss Carrington's good sense."

Jack, who had stuffed a cake into his mouth to keep himself from shouting at the fellow, choked on that, and had to bear the indignity of being whacked several times between the shoulder blades by the vicar before the viscount stopped choking and could breathe again. As soon as he could he waved the man away with an impatient hand, and sat frowning heavily at him.

"Sir," Lord Chalmsy said, "Despite your feeble protestations that you do not mean to be, I find you most insulting."

The vicar resumed his seat with a satisfaction Jack found utterly infuriating, and said calmly that sometimes the truth was bitter medicine to swallow. If that was true in the viscount's case the vicar was sorry for it, but he could not do less than speak the truth and provide the moral guidance it was incumbent that one in his position provide.

"The truth," Jack said, through clenched teeth, "is that if I were not tied to this bed, I would rise from it and heave you out the window with great good cheer! In fact, I may experience a miracle here and do just that!"

The vicar, paling slightly, rose from his chair and stood behind it as he said that perhaps the viscount had misunderstood, or he himself had been a bit overzealous in his concern for two ladies whom he held in the highest regard and in whose welfare he took a particular interest—

"And here's another truth for you," Jack said, his fists clenched tightly behind his head to keep himself from making better use of them. "Neither Miss Julia Carrington nor Miss Cressida Carrington need your protection from me— not that I think you could give it!—for I think highly of both, and would blacken the eyes of any man who dared impugn their honor."

The meaning of that was apparent; the vicar, after several stuttered starts, cleared his throat and said that well, yes, he was sure that was all very well, but he also was sure that the two of them could agree, as men of the world, that the world talked—

Jack, while very willing to agree *he* was a man of the

world, would not allow for the vicar being a man of *any-thing,* and said that he had always supposed it was the duty of the clergy to put *straight* any such talk.

Stonehall, who had become used over the years to controlling all conversations, wondered how he had lost charge of this one. He decided to take another tack and said, with a tight-lipped smile, "Perhaps you are not aware, my lord, of the high regard in which I hold Miss Julia Carrington."

Jack said icily that nothing the man had said in the last few minutes would indicate a high regard to him. Nor did he think Julia Carrington was in need of the vicar's high regard.

The vicar kept his smile pinned determinedly on his lips as he said, "Perhaps you are not aware that I often call upon Miss Carrington."

"The children have mentioned it," Jack said, sarcasm dripping from each word.

The vicar's lips tightened still further, for he had long suspected that Julia's brothers and sisters were not always as delighted by his visits as he was. He ignored the comment, however, as he continued.

"We have an understanding," Stonehall said.

"Oh?" Jack looked politely inquiring. "If Miss Carrington can understand you, she is even more remarkable than I had imagined. And I feel I should tell you I find Miss Carrington most remarkable."

The vicar, who did not believe he liked hearing that, looked suspiciously at the viscount as he said, his eyes narrowing, "You do not seem to understand, my lord. I find Julia Carrington to be a woman of unimpeachable character. Except for the fault of excessive levity—and the fact that she considers herself responsible for her brothers and sisters, despite my best efforts to instruct her that it is her mother and uncle who should bear the burden of raising them—I find her quite pleasing. She can keep house and dress a joint of meat, and sew a neat seam—"

He broke off at the look of astonishment on the viscount's face. "Was there something, my lord?" the vicar asked.

Jack blinked several times before responding. "Keeping house and sewing seams—these are the qualities you look for in a woman?"

Stonehall, surprised, nodded.

"And you think Miss Carrington's humor a *fault?*" Lord Chalmsy continued.

"A fault that I am sure can be overcome with proper instruction," the vicar assured him. "I have considered it at some length, and have decided so. I have even hinted to her that she should begin to work on the fault herself, but I realize that is not always an easy thing to do. Especially for a woman, for they are, of course, the weaker vessels."

The man looked so smug that Jack, goggling at the description of Miss Carrington as a "weak vessel," had to cough several times before asking, after a deep breath, "Are you telling me you are the one to instruct her?"

The viscount almost laughed as he pictured Miss Carrington's face when he recounted this conversation to her—for recount it he would, and he could hardly wait—but the laughter was driven from him by the vicar's next words.

"I am," the man said calmly. "For I intend to marry her."

Chapter
Nineteen

"You what?"

Viscount Chalmsy was halfway off the bed before he remembered his supposedly invalided state, and he fell back onto his pillows with a decided gnashing of teeth. First, he thought, he would like to throttle the vicar, who now sat smiling an odiously superior and smug smile, and then he would like to throttle Arabella, whose scheme to provide him with more time with Miss Carrington had so complicated his life that it was impossible for him to rise and throttle the vicar.

"I see I have surprised you," Stonehall said in that still-maddeningly calm voice.

Jack nodded and with great effort replied, "Is Miss Carrington aware of your plan?"

The viscount was pleased with his deceptively pleasant tone, and even managed a tight smile.

Stonehall smiled again, the smile of a self-important man not used to being refused. "I have not yet asked her, if that is what you mean. I thought it only appropriate to wait until her uncle returns home to gain his permission. I could, perhaps, apply to her mother, and of course, Miss Carrington is of age and I suppose there are those unschooled and underbred individuals who would propose my speaking directly to her. I, however, have always believed these things are best handled between men. Don't you?"

This time Jack was able to give a sincere grin, and he felt much more cheerful. In the few weeks he had known Julia Carrington it had been made more than plain to him that she was not a woman devoted to society's belief that men's rules should govern women's lives.

"I did not think you had asked her," Jack responded before he thought the words through, "for I am sure she would have sent you to the right-about quick enough. And what kind of a man who professes love for a woman is content to wait for a pair of gypsies like Julia's mother and uncle to return to take up their responsibilities—?"

He stopped when he saw the smile leave the vicar's face, and Stonehall's face darkened.

"I can understand that someone of *your* position and disposition would hold such intemperate views," the vicar said, biting off each word with a savageness that made Jack smile silkily. "But I do not believe Miss Carrington would be able to honor a man who spoke so vulgarly of *love,* and of her esteemed parent and uncle. Granted, their behavior is not what I condone, but they are her relatives, and when I tell her how irresponsible I find them, I do so in the most instructive manner possible. Although I have found her most prickly on that subject."

It occurred to Stonehall that this was not a topic he cared to discuss with Lord Chalmsy, who was regarding him with sudden interest. The vicar shifted in his chair before continuing. "I do, of course, hold Miss Carrington in high regard, and I have every reason to believe she will not be averse to my suit. I am, after all, the vicar, and while I do not like to puff off my consequence, I believe I can safely say I hold a position of some regard in this neighborhood. Which I'm sure you will realize is why I take it upon myself to speak to you so frankly."

Jack, unwilling to realize any such thing, snorted.

"*Every reason?*" Jack shouted. "You have *every reason* to believe she won't be averse to your suit? Are you daft, man? The children don't like you! Besides, you and Julia are so different that—that—" Jack saw the dislike and suspicion in Stonehall's face and ran a hand through his hair as, with great effort, he lowered his voice to say, "What might your reasons be, pray?"

"It would seem to me," the vicar said, regarding Jack closely, "that you take an unwarranted interest in my affairs."

"*Your* affairs?" Jack practically choked on the words. "*You* can go to China, for all I care!"

"Then," the vicar said, even more repressively, his florid face growing redder, "I can only assume you take what I consider an unwarranted interest in Miss Carrington's affairs."

Jack, who wanted to shout that there would be no affairs for Miss Carrington, because she was going to be *his* wife, and no one else's—certainly not a sour-hearted vicar's, who looked as if he'd swallowed a bottle of vinegar and never gotten over it—said, through clenched teeth, that he rather thought it was the vicar who took an unwarranted interest in—and reading of—Miss Carrington's *affairs*.

The added emphasis Jack put on the last word was not lost on the vicar, who glared heavily at the viscount and demanded to know just what business that was of *his?*

"And what business is it of *yours?*" Jack countered, furious with himself for not having a more stinging retort. Inwardly he was glad Miss Carrington was not there to see the two of them squaring off as if they were scruffy schoolboys or barnyard roosters; if this degenerated much further, he and the vicar would no doubt be taunting each other that each one's father was stronger than the other's.

Stonehall, struggling to remember his position as a man of the cloth, rose and said repressively that it did not appear to him that this discussion was fruitful, and he would take his leave.

"Good!" Jack said, glaring up at him. The vicar glared back.

"I hope," Stonehall said, with great meaning, "that you soon will be mended and on your way, my lord."

Jack's smile was silky, but his eyes snapped. "It is good of you to say so," he said, "but I fear your visit has set my recovery back at least a week. Perhaps two."

"Now, see here—" the vicar started, taking a step forward. He stopped as the door opened and Julia Carrington walked through it.

She was smiling, and started to say, "Mrs. Weston told me you were here," to the vicar, but the words trailed off as she looked from one to the other of the men, and back again.

"Is something amiss?" she asked as Lily came running into the room, shouting, "Jack! Jack! The most wonderful thing!"

The little girl was followed closely by William, who said, "Let me tell him, Lily! You got to hold it all the way home!"

Both children came to an abrupt stop when they saw Stonehall in the viscount's room, and their faces fell. Julia looked embarrassed, the viscount grinned, and the vicar, his brows drawn together, said, his tone unctuous (for he never was good with children), "And what is this wonderful thing you were about to tell the viscount? May I know, too?"

Lily took a step backward as William muttered it was nothing, really. Julia, even more embarrassed by the way the children made it apparent they did not appreciate the vicar's company, stepped behind them and, with a gentle hand on each child's shoulder, said, "Children, you have forgotten your manners. Make the vicar your best bow, now."

Both did, although their lack of enthusiasm was apparent. Jack's grin widened as the vicar's brows drew closer together.

"Well?" Stonehall said, frowning down at the children. "What is the wonderful surprise?"

Lily looked at the vicar, then up at Julia, who smiled and nodded encouragingly. "It's a kitten," the little girl said, looking down at the floor.

"Oh?" The vicar smiled condescendingly and said he rather thought Lily had a kitten already.

"Yes, but—" Lily began, the looked beseechingly toward Julia.

"A person may have more than one kitten," Julia said, smiling kindly down at her sister. The little girl beamed.

"You spoil these children, Miss Carrington." Stonehall's tone was austere, and he turned his attention to Lily and William, who were frowning fiercely at him for the remark. "You should be very glad Miss Carrington is your sister, you know," he told them. "Not everyone would let you keep another pet."

"Yes, well, I don't see why it's any concern of yours," William muttered, bringing a frown to the vicar's face and a warning squeeze on the shoulder from his oldest sister.

"William, apologize," Julia said.

"Well, it's not!" the little boy cried, lifting his eyes to her face. Julia, who agreed with him inwardly, still did not feel she could allow him to be rude to a guest, and was about to repeat her request that he apologize when Viscount Chalmsy unexpectedly entered the fray.

"He's right, you know," the viscount said, earning both children's gratitude. "It's none of the fellow's concern, after all."

"My lord," Julia said, shaking her head at the viscount. "You are not helping."

"Yes, he is," William said, and Lily nodded in agreement. The vicar said in even more austere tones that it was clear the viscount's presence had an adverse effect on the children.

"He does not!"

The viscount was both surprised and pleased by the way Lily and William took up the cudgels in his defense. William had stepped forward, his hands balled at his sides, and was glaring up at Stonehall. Lily, inspired by her brother's courage, also took a step forward and stood just behind William. She added her frown to the one her brother was directing toward the vicar.

"He has ever so good an effect on us," William said. "Just because he isn't forever prosing on at us, or acting as if we're great stupids, who must be told everything in the most conde—conde—"

The little boy looked appealingly toward Jack, who was pleased to supply "Condescending." The viscount aimed his own frown toward the vicar for good measure.

"That," William said, while Lily nodded. "And Jack—I mean, Lord Chalmsy"—William looked up at his older sister when he corrected himself—"is a great gun, and tells us the most exciting stories, and teaches us card tricks, and once drove his phaeton through a gate blindfolded—Edward told us—"

"Now, that is quite enough!" Julia, aghast that William had so far forgotten himself as to challenge their guest, continued, "William, apologize at once!" in a tone that brooked no argument.

Her younger brother looked beseechingly at up her, and then toward Jack. The viscount offered a small shrug and a commiserating look but, after a moment in which he met Miss Carrington's eyes, nodded agreement.

"Oh, very well," William said, kicking his toe into the carpet and staring down at the floor as he said, without looking at the vicar, "I apologize."

"Me, too," echoed the loyal Lily, who did not feel William should have to walk the path alone.

"Yes, well," Stonehall said, frowning at both children. "Did I but feel you meant it—" He happened to look up at Julia Carrington at that moment and read the condemnation in her eyes. It occurred to him belatedly that perhaps, as an adult, he should set a better example of gracious forgiveness than he was doing. He cleared his throat.

"We will speak no more of this," the vicar said, puffing out his cheeks. "Although I would suggest that you both apply yourself to your catechisms for an hour tonight and two hours tomorrow in an effort to acquire a little humility."

"And will you be reading your catechism too, vicar?" Jack asked, causing Lily to giggle and William to grin, although the boy manfully stifled a smile after a quick glance toward Julia.

The vicar cast Jack a glance of acute dislike before making Julia a bow that clearly said, "You see how it is."

Julia, who did see, frowned at Jack and said that she

would see the vicar out, which appeared to mollify the man a bit but which made Lord Chalmsy frown. That seemed to make the vicar feel even better.

"What a gudgeon," William said, after his oldest sister had ushered Stonehall from the room.

"He's more than that," Jack said, frowning heavily at the place where the man had just stood. "He's a—" He bit the word back as he realized Lily and William were regarding him expectantly, and grinned ruefully at them.

"Sometimes I forget myself," Jack excused.

"I like it when you forget yourself," Lily assured him. She seated herself at the foot of the bed, where she was joined by William, who nodded his vehement agreement. "It's ever so exciting. You're not like the vicar, who never forgets himself."

"I wish I could forget him," William muttered.

The viscount laughed. "Well, you can," he said. "And we will. Now, tell me what is so wonderful about this new kitten you've brought home."

"Oh, Jack!" Lily said, bouncing up on the bed and clapping her hands together. "Wait until you see it. It looks just like you!"

"*What?*" Jack didn't know if he should be flattered, but he was startled. No one had ever compared a feline to him before—at least, not that he was aware of.

"No, it doesn't," William said, frowning at his sister. "Not *just* like him. Jack doesn't have a tail, or four feet."

"You know what I mean!" Lily said, gazing at William in disgust.

"Well, Jack doesn't," the boy countered.

"Oh." Lily looked toward the viscount to confirm William's statement, and at Jack's nod she said, "What I meant was, he has eyes just like yours."

"Oh?" Jack's eyes widened, which made the children giggle. The kitten, they assured him, did the exact same thing whenever it was surprised. They had found it in the village, at the dressmaker's when Cressida stopped there for some ribbon. Mrs. Gibson, the dressmaker, had said she would be happy to have them take the little cat away, for, the children informed him solemnly, Mrs. Gibson said it was such a naughty thing.

"Well, that's another thing you and the kitten have in common," Julia said, shaking her head at the viscount as she walked back into the room. It was clear from the statement that she'd heard the children's earlier comments, and in spite of himself, Jack flushed.

"Lily, William, run and wash your hands now," Julia said. "We will be having our supper shortly. And afterwards you may bring the kitten up to show Lord Chalmsy."

"But Julia," Lily protested, "the kitten is *for* Jack!"

"What?"

Julia smothered the laugh that rose to her throat at sight of the viscount's face. It was clear from the way he said the word that this was an unexpected turn, and one not particularly to his liking.

Lily and William turned toward the viscount and nodded, smiling happily at him. "To keep you company," Lily explained. "So you will not be so lonely or bored here."

The viscount tried to tell them he was neither lonely nor bored, but the children clearly did not believe him. They would be both, they said, if they had to lie in their bedrooms with an injured foot all day, and if they were in such a situation a kitten would be what they would like above all things. They promised to bring the kitten up to him, complete with basket, as soon as dinner was over.

Jack looked appealingly toward Julia but realized he would get no help there; the lady of his heart wore a look that clearly said, "It serves you right."

"But Lily," the viscount tried, "I know how much you like kittens, and I would not wish to deprive you."

Lily beamed seraphically at him. "We *want* you to have this kitten, Jack—I mean, my lord," she assured him, looking mindfully up at her eldest sister. Then she startled both Miss Carrington and the viscount by throwing her arms around his neck and kissing him on the cheek. "We love you, Jack," she said softly as she pulled back.

Visibly undone, Jack patted her back awkwardly and said that he loved them, too—words he wished he could unsay as soon as he raised his eyes to Julia's face and saw the dismay there. Miss Carrington had gone quite white, and it was with considerable effort that she pulled herself together and said, "Come, children," shepherding Lily and William, who were unaware of the sudden tension in the room, before her as they departed. Lily and William both stopped at the door to peek around their sister and grin at the viscount, but Jack did not fail to notice that Julia Carrington left the room without a backward glance, or another word.

Chapter Twenty

Jack fully expected a visit from Miss Carrington that evening, and he was prepared to make the push to establish himself in her esteem by offering her his hand, his name, and—although it went against the grain to appear so romantically foolish—his heart, if need be. It was difficult for Jack to admit, even now, that he had discovered how much he cared about the woman, because Jack was used to keeping his heart intact and hidden. He had for so long held a part of himself back that the thought of offering all of himself—and possibly being rejected—made him so uncomfortable that he wondered for a moment if he could bring himself to the sticking point.

Then he pictured Julia's white face as he'd last seen her, and he knew that he must; at some point, since coming to Carrington Place, it had become of paramount importance to him to see that Julia Carrington be as untroubled and as happy as anyone could be. Somehow he must persuade her that it was quite all right for the children to love him, because he intended to be part of their lives forever; he did not intend to leave, no matter how adamant she was in her belief that he would. But how to convince her?

Worried as he was about that question, he was even more worried when he did not get the chance to answer it.

William and Lily tumbled into his bedroom carrying the kitten and its new basket bed as soon as they'd hurried through supper, and Edward and Cressida came a little later, to inquire anxiously what had happened. They told him they'd thought they were all to have a picnic in his room that night, but when they said that to Julia, they were told they must have misunderstood; Viscount Chalmsy was eating in his room and the Carringtons in the dining room, as they always did. They said Julia had sat without volunteering a word during supper, and when she was directly addressed, she'd answered quite at random, as if she hadn't heard the question.

Jack agreed that sounded very bad, but told them with far more confidence than he was feeling that he was sure when he and Miss Carrington talked, everything would be worked out and explained. Edward and Cressida looked as anxious as he felt, but he sent them off to bed saying that they would all have a good laugh over their worry in the morning. At that point he still believed he would see the eldest of the Carringtons that night, and he settled down to wait for Julia. She did not come.

To the viscount that seemed even more ominous than having her come to tell him to leave immediately. He slept little that night, only dropping into a troubled slumber shortly before dawn.

John, eyeing his master consideringly several hours later, gave it as his opinion that the viscount was looking considerably the worse for wear that morning. Upon being told somewhat acidly that Lord Chalmsy did not care to hear his opinion, not now, not ever, John grinned wide and said he was glad to see that this time the young lord was getting as good as he'd so often given. Jack glared at him.

"I have no idea what you're talking about," the viscount said untruthfully. "And even if I did, I'd thank you not to be so impertinent as to say it. Besides"—his glare increased as his faithful henchman grinned at him—"it's nothing of the sort."

"Oh?" John, in the process of sharpening the viscount's razor, paused and gave Jack a measuring look. "If it's not woman trouble, what is it?"

"Well, if you must know," Jack said, running a hand through his hair and frowning toward the foot of his bed, "it's that damned cat!"

"What?" John looked toward the kitten curled unconcernedly at Jack's feet, its tail covering the tip of its nose as it slept. The groom's lip turned up sardonically. "You'll have to do better than that, my lord," he said, "for I wasn't born yesterday, no matter how you seem to think it!"

"I'm telling you," Jack said, frowning at the slumbering feline again, "the little tyrant kept me awake all night! Mewing, and climbing onto my bed when it had a perfectly good place of its own in that basket the children made up for it! I must have put it back at least twenty times, and every time I'd turn over, there it would be again, snuggled up against me. The last time I got up to put it where it belonged it raced me back to the bed and jumped up onto my pillow before I could even lie down. I wanted to drop it out the window, but I'm sure Lily and William would notice it was missing, so at last I threw a pillow down to the foot of the bed and tucked the kitten under it. Rotten little pest."

One look at his groom's face told the viscount his servant did not share his view; John was openly grinning, and said he thought that while the kitten showed deplorable taste in who it was attracted to, it was a pretty little thing and the viscount should be happy to have it. "I'm sure your brother Charles will think so, too," John said.

Jack, remembering the unmerciful teasing he had given his brother when that gentleman was adopted by a wayward kitten, groaned. "You know, John," he said, "there is really no reason to mention the kitten to Charles. I can't see how it would ever come up."

"I can," John said frankly.

Jack's look was baleful. "What would it take for it *not* to come up?"

The groom thought a long moment, then grinned. "Can't think of a thing," he said, and began to whistle, cheerfully ignoring the viscount's glares and mutterings. The groom had just finished helping Lord Chalmsy into a fresh shirt when there was a soft knock at the door; Jack, thinking it must at last be Julia Carrington, said with what John considered a telling eagerness, "Come in!"

His face had brightened in anticipation, but it fell somewhat at the sight of Cressida Carrington coming through the door, accompanied by Edward. John, eyeing the young lady critically, concluded the viscount must have it bad if the sight of a young beauty so charmingly attired in a high-waisted gown of white cambric, fetchingly trimmed in soft blue ribbons, caused his face to fall. He was not allowed to voice that opinion, however, for the viscount dismissed him with a curt nod.

John, drawing his own conclusions, also nodded, and went off to the kitchen to have a cup of tea with Mrs. Weston, and to hear her speculations as to what was going on in the house at the moment.

Jack, thankfully unaware that he was the center of the servants' speculations, was frowning at Cressida and Edward.

He'd asked if they had talked with Julia, and received a negative answer. Brother and sister looked worriedly at each other and reported, in voices of great concern, that Miss Carrington had gone riding that morning. Alone. Shortly before dawn.

Jack, who had seen Julia ride out alone often, when she planned to remain on her own property or that of their neighbor Hartwell, and who had heard her praises as a horsewoman sung by her brothers and sisters more than once, gazed at them in puzzlement.

"Are you worried about her?" he asked, trying to understand why her riding out alone so concerned them today. "Do you fear for her safety? Do you think she has been thrown from her horse? Should we be looking for her, or . . ."

His words trailed off as the two regarded him in amazement.

"Julia?" Edward said. "Thrown?" He startled the viscount by starting to laugh. "Not she!" the younger man boasted. "Julia's the best horsewoman ever!"

"Well, yes," Jack said, confusion evident in his face. "I know you've said that, but if you're not worried about her safety, then what?"

The two exchanged glances again. "Julia has gone riding at dawn," Cressida explained. "Alone."

"Yes, you said that," Jack agreed, and waited. Cressida and Edward looked at each other again.

"The only time Julia goes riding at dawn alone," Cressida said, putting the words together slowly, "is when Mother or Uncle William have gone off on one of their jaunts again."

Jack, surprised to hear the girl's mother's and uncle's absences described as jaunts, blinked, and his brow furrowed. "I don't quite see—" he began.

"When she is sad," Edward explained. "And she doesn't want us to see."

"Oh." Jack sought an explanation other than his love's unhappiness. "Well, perhaps this time she just felt like riding."

Cressida shook her head at him. "I am sure Julia often feels like riding at dawn," she told him softly, "for she has said again and again that early morning is the freshest, most beautiful part of a day. But she never allows herself to do so, because there is so much else to be done. She only rides when she has completed her chores, which is why she rides so seldom, unless the riding is part of an errand or visit—there is always so much to do, she says."

Edward nodded in agreement. "Julia is troubled," he said. "Sad."

"Resigned," Cressida added with a sigh.

Her brother sighed, too.

Jack frowned at them both. "This obviously has a meaning for you that is beyond me," he said. "Would you care to explain further?"

Cressida looked at him, and Jack was aghast to see a tear roll down her cheek. "Julia," Cressida said, "is preparing to send you away."

"No!"

The word was uttered so forcefully that both Cressida and Edward jumped.

"No?" Cressida repeated.

Jack glared at her. "I am not some scruffy schoolboy," he told her, "and I am no longer *sent* anywhere. I have no intention of leaving Carrington Place until your sister has agreed to be my wife. I shall chain myself to the front pillars if I must, but she will be made to listen to reason. Dammit, she needs me! And I—" He stopped suddenly, staring from one startled face to the other for a moment, then said, the words quiet, "I need her."

Cressida and Edward were perfectly willing to agree, and Cressida added handsomely that she thought her sister would be very happy with the viscount—and the viscount very happy with her sister—could Julia just be brought to see that it would be all right for her to be so happy.

Unfortunately, Edward pointed out fair-mindedly, it wasn't his and Cressida's agreement that the viscount needed. It was Julia's. Lord Chalmsy had just agreed to that and sighed when Cressida, her brow furrowed, asked, "How will chaining yourself to the pillars help?"

Her brother glared at her.

"He doesn't actually plan to do it, Cressy," Edward said. "He just said it to show how determined he is."

"Oh." Cressida's gaze was tranquil as she regarded the viscount. "You could have just said you were determined," she informed him. "We would have understood that."

"Thank you, Cressida," Jack's tone was dry. "I shall remember that next time I care to make a point."

Edward rolled his eyes much as Jack had often seen Julia do, but Cressida smiled widely at Lord Chalmsy and said that she also hoped he would remember that her sister was bent on doing the right thing, and being noble, and he must convince her to follow her heart, above all things.

Jack frowned at her and snapped that there was nothing ignoble about marrying him.

"No, no," Cressida soothed. "But Julia will not wish to burden you with us—"

"Well, you wouldn't be a burden," the viscount said, frowning as he often did when offering a truth he was embarrassed to have come out of his mouth. "I've become rather used to all of you, and would miss you a great deal if I were to go away. I'd worry about you, too."

The viscount was rather appalled at what he'd said, thinking it might have bordered on the maudlin, but Cressida and Edward seemed to see nothing odd in it. They only nodded as Edward asked, with a practical air, just what it was the viscount planned to do.

"I am going to talk to your sister," Jack said, his face grim. "I am going to talk loud, and long, and persuasively. And if that fails, I'm going to—going to—"

"Yes?" Cressida said expectantly when he paused.

"I'm going to do something else," Jack replied. "My sister-in-law asked me to kidnap her to get my brother to propose; perhaps I'll do that with Julia."

"Kidnap your sister-in-law?" Cressida, puzzled.

"No, you silly chit!" her brother said scornfully. "Kidnap Julia!"

Edward paused, and shook his head slowly at the viscount.

"I don't think Julia would like that," Edward said.

"I don't think I'd like it either," Lord Chalmsy replied, with a great deal of truth but what Cressida considered a sad lack of romanticism.

"Julia has a strong temper," Edward continued. "And a pretty good left, when she chooses to use it."

Jack promised he would remember that, and sent them from the room with the expressed wish that they would usher their sister to him as soon as she returned from her ride. He settled himself as comfortably as he could on the bed—or as comfortably as a man who feels his life hangs in the balance of the next few hours could—and waited.

The kitten woke and demanded to be fed; that task was accomplished when Lily and William came to visit and to see how the viscount and his furry friend did. After eating, the little cat settled itself with great contentment on Lord Chalmsy's stomach and resumed its slumber. Jack frowned at it even as he absently stroked its soft fur, and waited.

And waited.

And waited.

At the same time the viscount waited, his brother, Charles Carlesworth, was driving toward Carrington Place at a steady pace. Anyone observing him as he went by might have surmised that Mr. Carlesworth was oblivious to the lovely morning, with its blue sky and light breeze, and in that they would have been right. Charles's thoughts occupied him as he drove along, and his thoughts were heavy and deep.

Upon returning to London the day before Charles had been astounded to discover his brother was not yet back in the city. There was something about the way his wife told the tale that made Charles suspicious, and under his continual prodding the sorry story did at last come out. Mr. Carlesworth was deeply shocked to hear that Jack was deceiving Miss Carrington in that manner, and he brushed aside his wife's assertion that it was with the purest of motives.

Arabella also had claimed that *her* motives in the matter had been most pure, something Charles was not at all able to accept, and the long and short of it was that they had had a huge row. Arabella had flounced from the room after telling her husband that he did not have a romantic bone in his body, and that she would not be speaking to him again for quite some time—at least until he apologized.

Since Charles could think of nothing for which he should apologize, but much his wife and brother had done that he considered wrong, he had shouted after her that that was just fine; he hadn't come back to London to talk to her, anyway.

It was, of course, untrue; Charles missed his wife and child immensely when he was parted from them, and he had returned to London as quickly as possible once the business he was commissioned to do for his grandfather was completed. It was just that he was shocked to the depths of his honest soul by Arabella's scheme to keep Jack at Carrington Place, and he was determined that his impetuous wife be brought to see the error of her ways.

If only, he thought wistfully as he drove along, he had a clue as to how to inspire her with that vision.

In the meantime, being a highly principled man, Charles felt the least he could do was remove his errant brother from Carrington Place as quickly as possible. With that noble mission in mind he had stormed into the hall of his grandfather's London town house and, under the amused eye of the earl, who had heard the raised tones of Charles and Arabella in the morning room and who had come from his library to enjoy the fireworks, slammed his hat onto his head with a curt command to the butler to have his man pack a change of clothes for him and have his phaeton brought round immediately.

His grandfather, following him out onto the steps, had pointed out the lateness of the day and suggested that Charles leave the following morning.

"You can't really burst in upon these people after dark,

dear boy," the earl had said with great good sense. "Suppose they've gone to bed. You'll no doubt arrive late, and they'll no doubt feel they need to offer you supper and a bed for the night. They're already putting up Jack; it seems to me our family already has imposed more than enough upon them."

"Don't tell me you approve of this—this—this unprincipled deception, too?" Charles had asked, astonished. His grandfather had immediately disclaimed any knowledge of an unprincipled deception, saying only that he thought it not the best of times to be leaving on a journey to the country.

Charles had said stiffly that he would spend the night at an inn and, his satchel arriving at the exact moment the undergroom brought his phaeton around the corner, he had stalked down the steps and climbed into the vehicle.

With a brief wave of farewell for his grandfather, who grinned and wished him a pleasant journey, Charles took the reins firmly in hand and raced down the street in style. The earl grinned broadly after him, then smiled at the feminine face peeking out of one of the front windows as Arabella watched her husband drive away.

Clangstone wished with all his heart that he could be there to see the sparks fly when Charles arrived to confront Jack, and Miss Carrington heard of the deception. His face brightened when he realized that if he waited long enough he would no doubt hear of them. He hoped he would hear from Miss Carrington, for everything Arabella had told him about the woman made him like her already.

On that happy thought the earl went back inside to wait for his great-grandson to wake from his nap so the two of them could accompany the boy's mother to Green Park. It was a daily outing Arabella had proposed after the earl had chanced to mention how he missed the green of the country, and it soon had become the highlight of the old man's day.

Charles was only two miles from Carrington Place when he rounded a bend that hid a small lake he remembered admiring when he first visited Jack after the viscount's accident. The water there was a perfect blue, surrounded on three sides by trees, and the spot offered a peaceful place to contemplate nature and life. Charles had almost driven past when he saw someone sitting at the water's edge on a large, flat rock. He recognized Miss Carrington and hesitated; after a moment he turned his phaeton toward the side of the road, tied his horses to a nearby tree, and approached her on foot.

The lady was obviously deep in thought, for she did not hear Mr. Carlesworth's approach until Charles was almost upon her; then she looked up, startled, and her startled expression grew as she recognized the newcomer.

"Mr. Carlesworth!" Julia said. "This is a surprise."

Charles made her a graceful bow, then stood for a moment regarding her with a seriousness Miss Carrington found alarming.

"I imagine you've come to see your brother," the lady said, trying to ease the gentleman's solemn expression. "I assure you he is quite all right; mending a bit slower than I might have expected, but in excellent spirits, and he does not complain of pain. I am sure your wife has told you it was the oddest accident."

At mention of his wife Mr. Carlesworth frowned. Julia, not knowing what to make of that, looked questioningly at him. Charles cleared his throat.

"Miss Carrington," the viscount's brother said gravely, "believe me when I tell you I would have come sooner, but

I just arrived back in London yesterday, and did not hear of this disgraceful situation until then. My wife"—Julia noted that Mr. Carlesworth frowned more heavily as he uttered the word—"has told me all about it, and I must tell you, I am deeply, deeply mortified."

"You are?" Julia looked at him in surprise, trying to understand his mortification. "Well, really, sir, there is no need. . . . And while your brother certainly did not appear *graceful* when he fell into the pond, I would not call it *disgraceful!* Although I have been sitting here wishing for the thousandth time that he had never come, that we had never met, that he had gone away that day, that he would never go away again—"

To Charles's considerable dismay the lady turned her head away from him and raised a quick hand toward her eyes, as if to wipe away a tear. When she turned back she was completely composed, although there was a sadness in her eyes that touched his heart.

She said, "I pray, sir, that you will ignore my last words. I am sitting here today thinking of things that never can be; it is a useless pursuit, I am persuaded, and one in which I do not usually engage. I think . . ."

What she thought Charles would never know, for her words trailed off. He goggled at her for several moments, then began. "My dear Miss Carrington, I did not realize! Can it be? Arabella said—but Arabella says so many things . . ."

He saw that the lady was looking at him in bewilderment, and cleared his throat before beginning again.

"Miss Carrington," Charles said, seating himself beside her on the rock and taking her hand into his so that she could not pull away, "I wish you would tell me what is in your heart. Can it be that you care for my brother?"

Julia tried to withdraw her hand, but the gentleman held fast; at last she shook her head and, looking away, said, "I cannot care for him, Mr. Carlesworth."

"Well, I don't blame you," Charles said frankly, "for a more rackety, quick-tempered, pig-headed fellow I have never seen. Although," the viscount's brother continued, trying to be fair, "he does have a good heart, and I must say that if I were ever in a real fix, there's no one I'd rather have on my side than Jack. For—"

It occurred to him that tears were once more running down Miss Carrington's averted cheeks. Charles reached hastily for his handkerchief and handed it to her, kindly accepting the muffled thanks she offered from its depths.

Watching her, Charles realized he had misunderstood her words; it was not that Miss Carrington *did not* care for his brother, it was that she felt she *must not*. Charles, who knew that feeling well, sighed.

He stared into space for several moments, remaining quiet as the lady composed herself. When it seemed her tears had slowed, he said, "You know, when I fell in love with Arabella I was miserable because I did not think I should love her. I felt it wouldn't work between us; I would be depriving her of opportunities if I were to ask for her hand. It did not occur to me that someone as lovely and as lively as Arabella could ever care for someone she had no trouble chastizing as 'a perfect stick' more than once—and I did not think she *should* care for me. I told myself time and time again that she should look much higher than a second son for a mate." He grinned sheepishly as Miss Carrington peeked up at him from the handkerchief's folds. "I thought I was being noble, you see."

Julia nodded, sniffing in sympathy. "I think it was very noble of you," she told him.

"Do you?" Charles considered that, his head tilted to one side. "Then perhaps Arabella was right when she said you and I are as alike as she and Jack are alike. Because I must tell you that Arabella says my being noble was a dead bore, and very hard on her nerves. She also says it was not right for me to try to make that choice for her, because she was the one who had the right to decide who she would give her heart to, not me. I imagine Jack feels the same about you."

He was relieved to see Miss Carrington had stopped crying, and continued. "Arabella got Jack to run off with her to bring me to my senses, you know."

"She did?" Julia regarded him in amazement. "Jack—I mean, Lord Chalmsy—told me that, but I thought he was exaggerating."

"Well, he probably was," Charles said, his head tilting the other way. "Jack likes to exaggerate. He probably didn't mention that my grandfather and Arabella's grandmother were with them the entire time."

Julia shook her head and smiled. "No," she agreed. "He didn't mention that."

Charles sighed. "We are a rather unusual family, Miss Carrington," he told her. "I have it on good authority that not everyone who elopes does it *en famille*."

The lady giggled before sitting up very straight and echoing his sigh.

"Mine, too, is an unusual family," she told him. "I have never really minded, until now, for the children and I get along well enough, and Father, although he was a second son without a large inheritance, managed to leave us well enough provided for that if I hold house, we get by. But now—now I fear we are *too* unusual."

She was looking away from him again and Charles said, his voice gentle, "Arabella says that your having an unusual family is all to the good, because then you won't be so shocked by the things we do." He shook his head, and this time his sigh seemed to come from his toes. "I must tell you, I find it quite tedious when Arabella is right about these things."

As Julia looked toward him, her eyes questioning, he explained. "She never lets me forget it, you see."

"But," Julia said, "I don't understand."

Charles's face was kind as he smiled at her. "My dear Miss Carrington," he said, "the first time I met you, you struck me as a woman of great astuteness. I think you do."

Pink tinged Julia's cheeks, and she put her hands to them in the most distracted way before she countered, "It is *you* who doesn't understand. I am responsible for my brothers and sisters. They depend on me. I should not have let it happen, but they have come to depend upon your brother, as well. I would not for the world want anyone, especially anyone like Lord Chalmsy, to feel that he must—must—"

She could not bring herself to say the words, and changed thoughts. "Besides, we do not live so retired here that I am not aware of what a shocking mésalliance the world would think he had made, were he to be so foolish as to ask me—" Once again she seemed to choke on the words, and paused for several seconds before continuing, her eyes staring out over the quiet lake. "The popular Viscount Chalmsy, with all his wealth and position, and a country miss with barely two pence to rub together! Oh, yes, they would say I had trapped him into marriage, had taken advantage of his accident! Oh, yes! It would be viewed as an accidental match, to be sure!"

"Oh." Charles's expression grew kinder, if possible, which made Julia wish to cry again. "Is that what you think, then?"

Charles smiled. "My dear Miss Carrington, let me tell you—and I am very serious about this—my brother Jack does as he pleases. He would *never* ask a woman to share his life because he thought he should, only because he wanted to."

"But he cannot want—" Julia protested. In spite of herself she could not still the catch in her voice.

"Miss Carrington," Charles said, smiling even wider, "I am appalled—and actually, as it turns out, quite pleased—to inform you that you are the innocent victim of a deception perpetrated by my unprincipled brother to get what he wants. That he has been ably aided by my equally unprincipled wife only appalls me further, and the only excuse I can give you for their actions—which I believe to be a paltry one but which I am sure they will both uphold to the last breath—is that they both have the purest of motives."

"What?" Julia was staring at him in bewilderment, her brown eyes wide.

"It is what Arabella says," Charles explained, "whenever she does something I do not quite like in her efforts to bring people together. She says she does it with the purest of motives. 'Leave them alone,' I tell her, 'stay out of other people's affairs.' But no. Arabella is a born matchmaker—a born meddler, actually—and she says sometimes people need a little push."

"A little push?" Julia repeated, her brow furrowed.

Charles looked at her and laughed. "In this case," he said, "she pushed Jack."

"I beg your pardon?"

"Into your pond," Charles explained. "It was a trick, Miss Carrington; my brother wished to stay at Carrington Place longer in the hope, Arabella tells me, that you would come to care for him as he cares for you. I told you Jack does what he wants, not necessarily what he should, and I believe both my brother and wife thought you did care for him more than you were willing to admit, and—and—"

"But he never said anything—well, hardly anything!— that would lead me to believe he cares for me, and—and—"

"Arabella says Jack felt it was too soon to say anything; that perhaps you did not care for him enough, or that you might not yet realize he would not leave you as your uncle and mother have so often done . . ."

His words trailed off, for Charles was appalled he'd said that. Mr. Carlesworth was not one to invade the privacy of another's family relations, and he didn't know where the words had come from. He was relieved, therefore, when the lady suddenly jumped from the rock to stand staring off at the water for a moment as she said, her voice astonished, "You mean—he *tricked* me?!"

"Yes," Charles agreed. "He did. I apologize for him. I believe it was very wrong of him, and you may be assured I shall tell him so shortly. But he did so because he loves you. You do love him, don't you?"

Mr. Carlesworth said the last words so anxiously that Julia, in the midst of trying to take in all she had just heard, stopped to stare at him before nodding slowly. Charles saw a look of wonderment spread over her face, and guessed it was the first time she'd acknowledged her feelings openly.

"Good!" Charles's face relaxed. "Because I cannot help telling you that there would be no bearing either him or Arabella for months if you did not. Jack would be so sulky, and would go off indulging in all the old excesses that make my wife anxious—and probably a few new ones, besides—and Arabella would be so sad. I will tell you to your face, Miss Carrington, that I am so hoping you will take my brother firmly in hand. I am, in fact, depending upon it. And I wish you much better luck than I have ever had with Arabella! Every time I think I am making progress, something happens and I realize we are right back where we started!"

"But it is impossible!" Julia cried, although something in her eyes implored him to disagree with her words. "He cannot really wish—he does not realize—oh, no! Our situations are too different! It is really quite, quite impossible!"

"My dear Miss Carrington," Charles said, taking her hand in his and raising it to his lips, "I have it on good authority from my wife that *nothing* is impossible!"

He paused to consider that, and frowned. "Except, perhaps, Jack and Arabella . . ."

So deeply was he pondering, his brow furrowed, that it was several moments before Charles realized Miss Carrington also was frowning. He looked at her anxiously.

"You *will* marry him, won't you?" he asked. At her look of hesitation he said, his face kind, "Do not be so noble, Miss Carrington, that you do not allow yourself to be happy. Or Jack. Or, from what Arabella tells me of their attachment to him, your brothers and sisters."

Julia thought for several moments before she raised an eyebrow and shrugged. "I am sure I should not even consider it, Mr. Carlesworth, but—oh, I must think! I must! And *he* must pay! He really must! How *dare* he trick me like that? When I have been so concerned, and so sad?"

She took several hasty steps away before turning to ask, her hands clasped in front of her, her face intense, "Mr. Carlesworth, will you help me extract revenge?"

Charles, loyal brother that he was, could make only one reply, and he did so promptly.

"With the utmost pleasure," Mr. Carlesworth said. "What must I do?"

Chapter
Twenty-one

When the knock on his door finally came it woke Jack from a sound sleep. He called "Enter!" groggily and sat up, belatedly aware that the kitten still slept upon his stomach. The little beast, unhappy at being so rudely awakened from its slumbers, uttered a *pffft!* to the room in general. It ignored Jack and the newest player on the scene as it stalked to the window overlooking the garden and settled itself on the sill with great dignity, staring out for a long moment before beginning a thorough wash that made it clear just how intently the small cat was ignoring the others in the room.

The newcomer, to Jack's amazement, was not Julia Carrington, but his brother Charles, who stood shaking his head at Jack with a condemnation Lord Chalmsy could not like— which he roundly told his brother. Charles appeared unmoved.

"What are you doing here, Charles?" Jack demanded. As sleep left him it occurred to the viscount that his brother was supposed to be away from London, and *not* at Carrington Place. "I thought you were in York."

"I returned from York yesterday," Charles said, the words measured. "I was more shocked than I can say to hear of your behavior in perpetrating this trick on Miss Carrington,

216

and left London immediately to fetch you. I must tell you, Jack, that I think it most unkind of you, to be deceiving Miss Carrington in this manner, when she has been so generous to you."

"Yes, well—" Jack wished Charles did not consider it quite so incumbent upon himself to tell Jack of his feelings. "It was Arabella's idea, you know."

Mr. Carlesworth frowned. "I have already told Arabella what I think of her involvement in this scheme."

"You have?" Jack paused to consider the implications of those words, then raised an eyebrow, his lip slightly quirked. "Took it well, did she?"

"Actually," Charles, always the truthful one, replied before he could stop himself, "she is not speaking to me, and tells me I have no romanticism in my soul."

He stopped abruptly and Jack, in the vain hope of distracting his brother with a really good quarrel, seconded his absent sister-in-law, saying that what she said was true; Charles was hopelessly unromantic.

Charles frowned at him. "We are not discussing me," he reminded the viscount. "And if you consider it *romantic* to deceive a lady you profess to love, to remain in her home under false pretenses, to encourage her brothers and sisters to aid you in your schemes and to take you to their hearts, when she has not yet told you if she is willing or unwilling to do the same—well, all I can say is that you have a pretty sorry idea of romance yourself."

It was clear his brother was warming to his topic and Viscount Chalmsy, not about to give his head to Charles or anyone else for washing, was formulating a stinging setdown when they were interrupted by the kitten. The little feline, having completed its toilette, had sat for several moments staring out the window in contemplation of the day. Suddenly it rose hissing, arching its back and scratching at the window as it continued to hiss and puff itself up until it gave the appearance of being twice its actual size.

"What on earth?" Charles asked as he and Jack stared toward the kitten.

"Here, now," Jack said, his voice sharp. "Stop that!"

The kitten ignored the viscount, and Charles, worried for the animal, walked toward the windowsill as he said it must be a bird or something that had so upset the little thing. At the window he stopped and said, in surprise, "Why, I think he's upset by what he sees below! Miss Carrington is seated on a bench, and some big fellow is kneeling at her feet, holding her hands—"

"What?"

Jack uttered an expletive Charles had not heard before and leaped from the bed. The viscount was beside his brother in two strides, and the sight that met Jack's eyes made him swear again. The viscount said, "Stonehall!" in a tone of such loathing that his brother could only stare at him.

Turning on his heel, the viscount quit the room in three long strides, leaving Charles gawking after him.

"But Jack—" Charles started, then smiled, and picked up the kitten. Stroking its fur softly, Mr. Carlesworth settled himself comfortably on the windowsill and completed his sentence in a near whisper. "Aren't you supposed to be invalided, Jack?"

The kitten, purring happily in the hands of someone who obviously understood the importance of scratching that certain spot behind its ears, did not even mind that the newcomer's arms shook slightly as the man laughed and said,

"You know, little kitten, I think this is going to be even better than we planned."

Then Mr. Carlesworth laughed again.

And laughed.

And laughed.

Jack, meanwhile, was charging down the stairs and through the hall, where he was met by Edward and Cressida.

"Jack, what on earth—" Cressida began, but the viscount ignored her. Brother and sister, seriously alarmed, followed him down the hall to the front door. As he opened it Lily and William tumbled through; it was clear they'd been on a mission and now, at the sight of the viscount standing before them, both shouted "Stonehall!"

Then they stared at their older brother and sister as Lily belatedly asked, "Is Jack all better, then?"

Edward and Cressida exchanged helpless glances, shrugged, and hurried through the door after Lord Chalmsy, the youngest Carringtons following them. All four heard Jack's roar of rage as he rounded the corner of the house and saw Miss Carrington struggling to extract her hands from the vicar's as that man tried his hardest to place fervent wet kisses in her palms. They rushed forward in time to see the viscount lift Stonehall by his collar and the back of his pants and toss him head first into the nearest flower bed.

It was, Lily and William solemnly assured Jack later, the finest thing they'd ever seen.

"*What,*" Jack demanded, glaring down at the stunned vicar and wishing the man would get up so he could knock him down again. "*do you think you are doing?*"

"What—what—" The vicar took a deep breath and shook his head as if to clear it. The action seemed to do so, for he suddenly returned the viscount's glare full force, and said, "How *dare* you?" in an indignant tone that made Lord Chalmsy invite him to stand so the viscount could to it again.

The vicar's eyes narrowed, and he said indignantly, "I am only doing what you suggested, after all."

"*What?*" Jack bent forward and clenched his hands at his sides to prevent himself from bloodying the man's nose in front of the children and Miss Carrington. "I never—"

"I told you I was waiting to ask Miss Carrington's uncle for permission to address her, and you said what kind of a man waits for such things, so I thought—I thought . . ."

His words trailed off in the face of the viscount's outrage.

Jack shouted, "*She's not going to marry you, you jack-anapes!*" as he stood over the flower bed, glaring down at the hapless Stonehall. The vicar was trying to inch away from the viscount without appearing to do so. "She's going to marry me, and I'll thank you to keep your hands off her, or I'll take your hands off *for* you, as well as your arms and other parts of your anatomy, believe me!"

Oblivious to the children cheering behind him, Jack turned toward Miss Carrington and pulled her to her feet, taking her hands in his as he shouted at her, too. "You're going to marry *me,* and there will be no nonsense about it! Do you understand?"

The way the lady raised her eyebrows made Jack think belatedly that shouting at the one you wish to marry is probably not the best way to go about becoming engaged. With an effort the viscount lowered his voice and repeated the statement. When it earned him no more response than a second quirked eyebrow he said, with a sudden burst of anxiousness that showed in his furrowed brow and troubled eyes, "You do *wish* to marry me, don't you?"

The lady's eyebrows rose further, and it seemed to Jack that they were in danger of disappearing from her forehead.

"Arabella said you did," he informed her, talking fast, his usual sangfroid gone. "But you just didn't know it yet. And Cressida and Edward—they said it, too. And they said it would be a very good thing, which it would. It's as if everyone knows it but you, and I have been most patient, waiting for you to sort it out. But my patience is at an end and you must say you will marry me *now,* because I cannot bear it another moment if you do not. And I will not take no for an answer."

Miss Carrington, who had made a choking sound when his lordship spoke of his patience, turned her consideration toward the brother and sister he had named. Both shifted uneasily from one foot to the other under her reproachful gaze and looked more guilty than they liked.

"That is . . ." the viscount said, his voice growing uncertain when the lady still did not speak, "I think . . ."

He stopped at Miss Carrington's firm request that he let go of her hands, and dropped them as if they suddenly had become hot coals. He flushed when she followed her request with the acid comment that she did not believe he thought at all.

"But Julia," Cressida's soft voice was anxious, her face worried as she stood watching them. "You do love him, don't you? You *did* go riding alone this morning, and you had to add the household accounts three times, you were so distracted yesterday, and you hum in the library all the time, as I haven't heard you do since before Father died, and you're doing your hair more carefully than you ever used to, and you had the dressmaker make up that green silk gown—"

Julia turned and stared at her sister for several moments— just stared—before asking in a thoughtful voice if Cressida didn't have someplace else to be—if they didn't *all* have someplace else to be. When none of her brothers and sisters seemed able to think of such a place she recommended that they all find one.

Immediately.

With great reluctance the four younger Carringtons exchanged glances, turned, and started slowly away. They took turns looking back, just in case Miss Carrington changed her mind, or something exciting happened.

"Oh. Take this fellow with you," the viscount called after them, giving Stonehall's shoulder a far from gentle shove as he urged the man to follow the children. The vicar had risen during Cressida's speech and was engaged in brushing off the worst of the dirt clinging to his clothes.

"Now, see here," Stonehall started, read the threat in the viscount's eyes, and said sullenly that very well, he would go—unless Miss Carrington wished him to stay?

He said the words so expectantly that Julia, aware of the shock it would be to him, did her best to soften her denial with a smile. It did no good.

When she shook her head the vicar's face grew stern and he said that, well, then, there was no accounting for taste, and he was sure that he wished her very happy, although he doubted she would be, and he would do his best to put this whole unfortunate episode behind him, although the folly he was seeing would make that very difficult, and no doubt would provide much fodder for his sermons in the coming months.

It was clear that he would have said more, but Lord Chalmsy took a meaningful step forward and the vicar departed with an air of deeply offended dignity.

"Good riddance," Jack said with satisfaction when the man disappeared around the corner. "Now, then."

He turned back to Miss Carrington, the smile on his face turning to a look of dismay when he saw that the lady had sunk back onto the garden bench and sat with her face averted from him. Her shoulders shook and her face was pressed into a handkerchief that showed a generous border of lace.

Jack, aghast to see her cry, was beside her in an instant. He tried to take her into his arms, but the lady resisted.

"Here, now," Jack protested, trying to understand her tears. "You surely aren't sorry to see that old windbag go?"

Miss Carrington heaved a heartfelt sigh. "But he wished to marry me." She seemed to choke the words into her handkerchief, which was pressed over most of her face. "Who will marry me now?"

"Well, I told you," the viscount said, running his hand through his hair in a most distracted way even as he tried to take her into his arms again. "I will."

He coughed when the lady's elbow came in sharp contact with his ribs, and he left off trying to embrace her in favor of hugging his side.

"The vicar," Miss Carrington pointed out, her words muffled as she still turned her face away, "did not *tell* me. He *asked* me."

"Oh." Jack considered that a moment, then patted her back awkwardly as he said, "Will you marry me?"

"The vicar," Miss Carrington whispered into her handkerchief, just loud enough for him to hear, "asked me on his *knees*."

"Now, see here—" Jack could feel his temper rising. He did his best to restrain it as he remembered Charles had just told him that Arabella had accused Jack's brother of not having a romantic bone in his body. The viscount, known in London as a favorite with the ladies, rolled his eyes at his own ineptness and, not wanting to find himself in company with his brother, grimaced. Then he dropped to his knees.

Taking one of Miss Carrington's hands in his, the viscount said, in the most romantic voice possible, "Miss Carrington—Julia—will you marry me?"

He was not sure just what he expected at that moment, but the one thing he did *not* expect was to have the lady suddenly rise and push him backwards. As he lay sprawled in the dirt, gazing up at her in surprise, it became blindingly clear that Miss Carrington had not been crying. Truth be told, Jack detected a great deal of anger in her eyes. He tried hastily to rise, only to be tripped and pushed back again.

"How *dare* you?" Miss Carrington shouted. "How *dare* you deceive me in this way?"

"Deceive—" Jack started. He glanced up toward the window of his bedroom and saw Charles standing there, obviously enjoying the scene. Jack glared at his brother, and the glare bespoke vengeance. It incensed him when Charles laughed.

"He told you, did he?" Jack said, returning his gaze to the lady.

"Yes." Julia nodded. "I am relieved to find there is at least one person of integrity in our—I mean your—family."

She made the correction quickly but the viscount, about to protest that he had a great deal of integrity, heard it. He instantly gave over on the honesty issues to say eagerly, "You said '*our*'. You did, I heard you. That means you are going to marry me, doesn't it? *Doesn't it?*"

He again started to rise, but Miss Carrington stopped him by the simple expedient of pushing him off-balance and placing a foot on his chest.

"Now, see here—" Jack said, frowning at her.

The lady frowned back, her gaze every bit as fierce as his.

"No," she said. "*You* see here. I know it is absolutely foolish and irresponsible and probably quite bad of me, but if you truly do wish to marry me, after all I have to say to you, then yes, I will marry you. *But*—" She pressed down with her foot as he once again tried to rise. "You will hear me out, and you will agree to my terms first. Do you understand?"

"Terms?" the viscount repeated. He frowned, for he did not like the sound of the word. Miss Carrington nodded.

"Terms," she said. "And the first one is, there will be no more deceptions. Not even those"—she remembered Mr. Carlesworth's words—"done with the purest of motives. Agreed?"

Jack, with a darkling glance toward his brother, still standing in the window laughing down at him, nodded.

"And you understand that the children will be living with us until they are grown."

"*Of course* the children will live with us! I am only marrying you so that the children will live with me!"

Miss Carrington shook her head at him, refusing to be drawn. "The vicar," she told him, her lips prim, her eyes alight, "would be the first to tell you that such levity is unbecoming in a person of your stature."

Jack grinned. "Is that all?" he asked hopefully.

The lady shook her head again. "You must also realize that my mother and uncle will be moving in and out of our lives, and they must always be welcome wherever we are."

Jack thought a moment. It seemed to him that the two had too often moved in and out of Miss Carrington's life, and he did not care to encourage them. "How often?" he asked.

"As often as they wish," Miss Carrington said, voice firm.

With an optimism he had not heretofore known he possessed, Jack decided that probably wouldn't be too often. He agreed.

"You must understand," Miss Carrington said, her voice suddenly anxious as she gazed at him as if trying to read his thoughts, "that I like living in the country, and I think it is good for the children to be here. I will want to spend a great deal of time outside of London. Does that trouble you?"

Jack said that he had grown quite tired of the city, and looked at her expectantly. "Next?"

"You mustn't think that I will not be speaking my mind," Miss Carrington told him, a resolute expression on her face, "for I will. And I will not be browbeaten or cowed, no matter how hard you try."

"I never try to browbeat anyone!" Jack replied, with complete disregard for the truth. The lady looked at him—just looked at him, her eyebrow quirked—until he at last looked away. After a moment the viscount said, his tone sulky, "Oh, very well. What else?"

Miss Carrington hesitated. "You do understand," she said at last, removing her foot and looking down at her lacing and unlacing fingers as he rose with alacrity, grateful for the chance, "what people will say, don't you?"

"I imagine they will say 'that lucky Jack,'" he told her.

Miss Carrington shook her head, taking a deep breath before raising her eyes to his. "They will say you have made a shocking mésalliance," she told him, her eyes anxious. "The whole world will say so."

"Hang the world," Jack said promptly.

"But—"

"Julia, please. Has it ever occurred to you that they will say *you* made a *brilliant* match?"

He affected such a superior, self-satisfied pose that the lady, despite her best efforts to be serious, could not help but laugh. At that sound the viscount relaxed. He captured her restless hands to hold them tightly in his own, and said with great tenderness, "They will be wrong, of course. It is *I* who have made the brilliant match—as I am sure Arabella will tell anyone and everyone she can!"

He said the last words with some irritation, and Julia laughed again.

"Well, then," she said, "if you agree to my terms there is really only one more thing I must tell you."

Jack watched her laughter give way to great seriousness and he took a step back, letting go of her hands. He took a deep breath and plunged his own hands deep into his pockets, prepared for the worst. "What is it?" he asked.

"I must tell you that I will love you with all my heart," Julia said softly, a tentative smile growing on her lips and spreading to her eyes, "for as long as I live, if you only will love me in return."

The viscount did not vouchsafe a word, but the way he took her into his arms and held her as if she were the greatest gift ever given, his lips coming down to touch hers with a tenderness and then a passion borne of love, seemed enough answer for her, and the lady was content.

* * *

Two hours later, as Charles sat alone in the morning room, sipping a cup of tea provided by the thoughtful Mrs. Weston, he heard the sound of a carriage drawing up out front. He smiled and rose in time to look out the window and see his wife descending from it like a small whirlwind. She rushed up the steps but he was before her, opening the door before she even had time to raise the knocker.

"Charles!" she said, staring up at him.

"Arabella," her husband returned. The lady glared at him.

"I am not speaking to you, Charles," his wife announced, sweeping into the hall and looking anxiously around, "but if I were, I would tell you that I think it is despicable that you came here to tell Miss Carrington about our tiny deception—you *did* tell her, didn't you?"

She looked hopeful, then crushed, when he nodded.

"It is too bad of you, Charles," Arabella said in the tragic tones her husband believed could earn her a place on the stage. The lady took several steps toward the window and stood staring pensively out it. "If you have ruined everything, I will never speak to you again—which I would tell you if I were speaking to you, which I'm not."

Standing behind her, Charles smiled. He did so love this woman!

He moved forward to take her hand, and, with a finger to his lips, led her toward the long double doors that separated the morning room from the steps to the garden. Looking out, they saw Lord Chalmsy walking arm in arm with Miss Carrington. The two were surrounded by Miss Carrington's siblings and, as they watched, the viscount stopped to drop a warm kiss on his betrothed's forehead.

"Well!" Arabella said, clapping her hands together, her

anger at her husband forgotten. "Didn't I tell you they were made for each other, Charles? Didn't I? Wasn't I right?"

She looked so triumphant and so happy as she gazed up at him that her husband could see nothing for it but to follow his brother's example and to kiss his own beloved's forehead. "Yes, my dear," Charles said. "You certainly did."

Harmony restored, they stood for some time, arms intertwined, both smiling contentedly at the happiness they felt and saw before them in the garden.

*If you enjoyed this book,
take advantage
of this special offer.
Subscribe now and get a*

FREE
Historical
Romance

No Obligation (a $4.50 value)

Each month the editors of True Value select the four *very best* novels from America's leading publishers of romantic fiction. Preview them in your home *Free* for 10 days. With the first four books you receive, we'll send you a FREE book as our introductory gift. No Obligation!

If for any reason you decide not to keep them, just return them and owe nothing. If you like them as much as we think you will, you'll pay just $4.00 each and save at *least* $.50 each off the cover price. (Your savings are *guaranteed* to be at least $2.00 each month.) There is NO postage and handling – or other hidden charges. There are no minimum number of books to buy and you may cancel at any time.

Send in
the Coupon
Below

To get your FREE historical romance fill out the coupon below and mail it today. As soon as we receive it we'll send you your FREE Book along with your first month's selections.
